Don't Fade.
Breathe Easy.

~

By Sarah Delany

Graphic Design (Cover) - Michael Pati Fuiava

Editing and Proofreading - Rebecca Andrews

Dedication

To Jonathon McGrath, my big bubba,

I wish you would have stayed.

My soul will be forever missing a piece because you are gone.

Keep that piece safe and treasure it. It helps me to know wherever you are that a part of me is with you always, until we meet again.

Not a day goes by without you crossing my mind.

Loving you from afar,

Your lil bubba

xxx

Contents

Chapter 1

-- Tamsyn --

Stinging, cold rain pelts down on me while I'm stuck in the same spot, frozen and unable to move. Am I dreaming? This can't be real, can it?

The male police officer throws a worn, grey blanket over my shoulders but the chill runs too deep. I can't get warm. Shivers take over my body and I can't get them to stop. I stare off into the distance long after the ambulance lights disappear from view. He asks for my address and I prattle it off, my mind elsewhere. The female police officer comes and puts an arm around me. My feet thaw, allowing me to be directed to their car with her guiding hand. She buckles me in, my mind too occupied to deal with menial tasks. My sole focus is on the broken boy they took away.

The rain still pours down as she helps me out of the car, leading me to my front door. I open it and go inside and my mum is there, looking like she just arrived home. Her concern leaks out of her as she rushes to me, cupping my face in her hands. Lifting my gaze to hers, I'm unsure what she sees in my eyes. I try to communicate with my eyes, words won't come. How do I voice what happened? She's talking to the officers but I can't hear anything they say. They hand her a card before they leave and then it's just me and Mum.

"Bub, talk to me please. What happened? Who was with you?" her worried voice pierces through the fog. I can feel the burning tears leaking down my blank face. I can't tell her though. If I voice the words then it makes it true. My body is still racked with shivers. Why won't it stop? My heart speaks and puts into words what I need right now.

"Tate please, Mum," I mumble out, and my mum understands.

"How about we get you changed first bub? You're shivering," she tries to tug the grey blanket from around me.

"No," I yell. "Tate please?" I beg, needing him to help hold me together. She lets out a sigh as she shuffles me out the door, helping me into the car. She knows where JP lives so she drives there without me having to give directions. With her arm firmly wrapped around me, she leads me up to the door and knocks. Shivers continue. JP's dad answers the door with a smile but his face drops as he takes in my dishevelled appearance and my soaked through clothing. Cotton wool blocks all sound again and I see his lips move but can't hear what he's saying. A second later, JP and Tate are pushing around him to get to me.

Their wide eyed stares take me in and Tate instinctively lifts me in his arms, bundling me in his embrace as he moves to sit on the couch.

"What happened?" I hear the panic in his voice, but I can't tell if his question is directed at me or not. I stare at the wall. My blanket gets removed and is replaced with a towel. I can feel them all lingering around me. Tate presses my head against his chest and I listen to his heart hammering away under his skin. Thump, thump, thump. I'm ready to wake up from this nightmare now, I can't stay here any longer.

JP's face comes around the back of the couch and he reaches over and takes my hand in his, squeezing it tight. JP and Rafe. They're a pair. I squeeze my eyes shut knowing what I need to do. JP is Rafe's best friend. He will need him now. I just wish I wasn't the one who had to break his heart.

"Rafe," is all I manage to croak, my throat raw. JP's brows knit confused.

"You want Rafe?" JP asks, and I feel Tate's arms loosen around me. I shake my head but I can't find my voice.

I hear my mum's voice catch as she says, "Oh my God." I close my eyes, wet warmth floods down my face as my mum tells them what she knows. "The police said a boy was taken away in an ambulance. Tamsyn gave him CPR, saving his life. Was it Rafe, bub?" I can only nod as the tears stream down faster.

"Why were you out there again? Is he okay?" JP yells at me.

"JP shut it, man. Leave her alone," Tate sternly says to JP. JP runs a hand through his hair. I can feel the anger pulsing through him, directed at me. I don't blame him. He assumes it was me out there on the dock and Rafe came to my rescue. I don't know if I have it in me to tell him the truth. To share Rafe's secret.

"Rafe," I cry into Tate's chest as he wraps me tighter in his arms. Tate. Oh no. How will this affect him? Will it send him into a panic attack because of Quinn?

"It's okay Sweetness, I got you," Tate whispers to me. I breathe in his earthy scent, letting his strength seep into me while my mum talks with JP's parents. I watch JP stride back and forth with worry for his best friend but he doesn't know the whole truth. Why did Rafe call me? I don't know what the right decision to do is but if I keep this inside, I fear it'll break me. Rafe needs help. I stop second guessing myself and shrug out of Tate's hold. JP needs me now.

He stops in his tracks, facing me with worry. I leap into his arms, wrapping my arms around his neck and he hugs me close, unsure.

"I'm sorry JP," I cry.

"It's okay. I'm sorry I got angry," he says, but he doesn't understand. The room is quiet now, our parents watching our embrace. I can feel Tate behind me. I can't look at his face, knowing I will see uncertainty there. I close my eyes, gather my courage and breathe out.

"It wasn't an accident," I whisper so JP can hear, his body stilling against me.

"What do you mean?" he says, as he leans back to look at my face. I release his neck and step back from him and into Tate's strong embrace. With his arms around, he provides me safety and strength without realising it. I wring my hands, looking at the floor. "What do you mean?" he asks again. With tears in my eyes I gaze up at him and break his heart.

"I think he did it on purpose JP." He stares at me with furrowed brows still not understanding. Tate wraps his arms around my waist. His presence is all I need to continue so I rush the words before I can stop myself. "He rang me and said he was sick of being strong and wanted some peace. He said he figured out how to find it then he said goodbye. I ran all the way to the dock and found him in the water," I say as the haunting images surface in my head so I burrow into Tate's chest.

"John," I hear his dad yell as he rushes to catch JP before he hits the floor.

"He wouldn't. He wouldn't do that," JP mumbles as we stare at him with his knees bent and his body folded over them. "Rafe's the happiest person I know, he just wouldn't," he continues, but I have no words to comfort him. I feel Tate stiffen behind me, his breaths becoming shallow. He lifts me up in his arms, my legs automatically wrap around his waist and he carries me back to the couch. He nuzzles his face into my neck, breathing deeply. His tremors intensify so I squeeze him harder, hoping he can calm himself.

4

Chapter 1

"I'm here Tate, I've got you," I whisper to him so only he can hear. He's trying to keep himself together when his mind is probably riddled with horrible thoughts. All I can do is hold him, hoping he can hold himself together. I hear my mum talking with JP's mum.

"I better ring Rafe's mum. By the sounds of it, they won't know what's happened," JP's mum says. She leaves for a minute then returns with unshed tears in her eyes. "I couldn't do it over the phone, but they're home so I'm going to go over there," she says to JP's dad.

"I want to go to Rafe," JP says from the floor where he hasn't moved from.

"Come on son, get up and I'll take you to the hospital while your mum goes to see Rafe's parents. You want to meet us there, dear?" he says to his wife, which she nods to.

"Tamsyn, honey how about you come home?" my mum asks, bending down to get a glimpse of my face fiercely nuzzled into Tate's neck. I shake my head.

"I'll look after her Tanya, if you don't mind her staying here?" Tate's shaky voice asks, as he looks up at her.

Mum rubs my back before asking, "Why don't you both come home with me then?" but I shake my head. Memories of sleepovers and Rafe smiling at me in my room surface and I squeeze Tate tighter, shivers taking over my whole body. My mum must notice as she says, "Okay love, stay here but Tate please ring me if you need anything. Do you want me to drop some clothes back for you, bub?"

"That's ok, I can give her some Tanya," Tate says. My face stays firmly in the crook of Tate's neck, breathing in his scent. I hear them moving around me but I can't look at any of them. I'm drained and my body won't stop shaking. My mum plants a kiss to the side of my temple as she squeezes my arm before she leaves. I block out what JP's parents say to Tate, I can't focus on that. It's as if my mind is conserving energy only focusing on one thing at a time. I'm unaware of where JP is either. The thought of his face has me whimpering which I try my best to contain.

I hear the door click as Tate and I sit still on the couch, breathing each other in. Both shaking but unable to do anything else to comfort the other. Time escapes me, I'm not sure how long we stay there, silent and unmoving. Tate's breaths steady as he gains control of himself. He's stronger than I realised, holding himself together and not falling apart in front of JP and his family. He's come a long way.

"Sweetness?" he softly says, as his head moves. His gentle hands lift my gaze to his. My blurry vision tries to focus on him. I see my own pain reflected in his eyes. He wipes his thumb softly against my cheek, clearing the lone tear that escapes. "Sweetness, you keep shivering. Do you want to take a shower?" I shake my head, I don't want to leave the safety and warmth of his arms.

"I'll come with you," he says, reading my mind as always. He knows I don't want to let go of him yet. With me clinging to him like a spider monkey he stands up, carrying me to the bathroom. My face is firmly planted back into the crook of his neck as he opens the glass door, turning the shower on. I don't think I can let go of Tate so he doesn't give me the choice. He waits for the water to warm, then he steps into the shower with me clinging to him. The warm spray rains down on both of us, our clothes plastering to our skin.

Letting the warmth seep into me, my shivers finally subside. I release my head from Tate's neck and lift my eyes to his. All I see in his gaze is his worry for me. Always me. He always puts me before himself. My heart makes my body react and I press my lips to Tate's. I need to feel something other than the despair and hopelessness I'm feeling right now. It takes a hesitant second but then he's kissing me back. His hand slides down the side of my face, wiping my soaked hair away from my cheek where it clings.

Our lips move in a frenzy, hungry for each other. Hoping his kisses can heal the pain, I beg for more and he returns it just as hungry for me.

He turns and presses me into the shower wall. The cold tiles shock me as he pushes his body into me, holding me up. My legs clench around him, holding him to me as he lets go, one hand sliding into my hair as his kisses move down to my neck. I arch my face upwards, giving him more access.

His other hand moves, gripping my butt tenderly. Pressing himself into me I feel his hard length rubbing against my core. I gasp at the sensation, locking my eyes on his. We've never been this frenzied for each other but when I search his eyes I see pain. If this is what we need to drown out the pain we are both feeling, I'll take it. I give a slight nod to let him know it's okay. He captures my lips again as he grinds himself into me.

We both get lost in each other. As he has me pressed to the wall, I struggle to pull my drenched shirt over my head. Holding my gaze, he presses his body harder into mine, holding me against the tiles while he pulls his own shirt off. I run my hand down his chest feeling his firm muscles. His hand trails a path down my neck, leaving a burn where he touches. He palms my breast gently, swiping his thumb over my hard nipple protruding through my bra. He swallows my gasp, his tongue finding mine. I bring my hands back around his neck drawing him closer to me, trying to meld our bodies together.

A few minutes pass until we pry ourselves apart. Heavy breaths fill the space between us, as he lowers his forehead to press against mine. Eyes closed and hearts galloping, we catch our breaths. He grips under my butt and twists so I'm under the stream, warming me again from the cold slowly seeping in from the tiles. He delivers a chaste kiss to my lips as he lowers me to my feet. I don't want the pain to creep in though, just wanting to forget for a minute. I unclasp my bra, but Tate stops my hands and holds my gaze.

"Not like this baby," he softly says, causing my eyes to burn as the tears start falling. The unwelcome sobs start as he draws my head to his chest, holding me tight. He reaches behind me and turns the water off. Picking me up again as my cries wrack my body, he steps out of the shower and grabs a towel, wrapping it around me. He carries me back to his room and plants me on my feet, rubbing the towel over me, drying me. "I need to get you some warm clothes. Can you stand?" he asks, as he lifts my chin up. I nod as I hold the towel to my chest.

He steps over to his drawers, pulling clothes out and placing some on the bed for me. "I'll let you get changed. I'll change in the bathroom," he says, as he quickly leaves. My trembling fingers remove my bra and drag my soaked underwear off. I pluck Tate's t-shirt off the bed, shrugging it quickly over my head. I pick up the sweatpants he's left too and pull them on, tying them as tight as I can. They're still loose so I roll the top of them over a few times, hoping it'll hold them in place. I sit on the edge of the bed waiting for him.

It isn't long before he returns, probably not wanting me to be left alone for long. He's got our wet clothes from the shower with him so he picks up my underwear and disappears again for a minute before returning, empty handed. He sees me sitting there, grabs the towel from the floor and dries my hair. The sobs return. It reminds me of when Rafe dried my hair after my breakdown in the shower. Rafe. For a second I had forgotten, had pushed thoughts of him aside but now they flood back in. Tate gathers my shaking body in his arms and pulls the covers back so we can get in, covering us with them. His bedside lamp illuminates the room as I cuddle in as close to him as I can while he holds me together, letting me fall apart.

"Let it out baby," he says, as the tears stream down my face, soaking his shirt. He holds me until my sobs quieten, my body drained. Behind closed eyes, I bring his green eyes to mind and hold them there but the honey brown eyes of the smiling boy try to penetrate through. Tate holds me tighter as if he can tell my mind is forcing me to see things I don't want to. My ear to his chest, listening to the thumping of his heart is how I manage to drift off and forget for a minute how devastating and bleak my world is at the moment.

Chapter 2

-- Tate --

I hold my broken girl so tightly in my arms until her breaths even out and I'm sure she's asleep then I release my grip slightly. The storm still rages outside, raindrops tinkering against my window. I reach out flicking the lamp off, encasing us in darkness. I scrunch my eyes shut, keeping my breaths under control. Rafe. I can't believe it. I should have seen it coming. I should know the signs. Me more than anyone should have known.

Thinking of Rafe brings thoughts of Quinn into the mix. Don't think. Don't think. Don't think. I thought I might be finished with my mantra but it seems I'm going to need it a bit longer. Images of Tamsyn when she arrived at my house flood me. It was like going back in time to when she had her breakdown in the shower. She looked so broken and defeated. For a second when she said Rafe's name, I thought she was crying out for him instead of me. Seeing her jump into JP's arms, my heart splintered. Jealousy spiked in me realising she needs the guys as much as they need her now. What did I expect to happen when I left her and wouldn't return. I pushed her away and I should be thankful the guys were here for her. It still hurts though.

As soon as my mind caught up to what she told JP about Rafe, my breath caught. Not again I thought, not again. I don't think I will survive losing someone else to suicide. With her in my arms, I managed to dig deep and keep myself from having a panic attack. I let us get out of control in the shower though, needing her to strip away the pain. As soon as she went to take off her bra I knew I needed to stop this. I didn't want our first time to be shrouded in pain and hurt. I hope she realises that's the only reason I stopped it.

I don't know if I'll be able to sleep tonight, not with all these thoughts swirling through my mind. Exhaustion managed to pull Tamsyn under but how long that will last I don't know. Lying in the dark I get lost in my thoughts and it isn't until I hear the front door slam shut that I'm pulled from them. I loosen my arms from around Tamsyn and quietly step out into the hall, careful not to wake her.

"John, calm down son," my uncle says to JP. I walk into the lounge and find JP with his fists clenched, staring at his mum and dad. His parents look wrecked. My aunty's eyes are bloodshot from tears. I step quietly to the side of JP, his head whips up to meet my stare and I see the anger and hurt lacing his eyes.

"What happened?" I ask quietly. "Is he okay?"

JP huffs angrily, "I wouldn't know, he didn't want to see me." He runs a hand through his dishevelled hair like he's been doing it all night long. "I'm his best friend and he wouldn't even see me," he says, his voice cracking at the end. That's why he's angry. He wanted to be there for Rafe and Rafe wouldn't let him.

"Tate, is Tamsyn still here?" my aunty asks me, leading my eyes to her voice. I nod.

"Yeah, she fell asleep a little while ago," I tell her.

"Did she say anything?" JP asks, his anger fading.

"No, she didn't say anything else after you guys left. She's been crying the whole time," I tell them.

"Shit," JP curses. "Shit, shit, shit," he continues, his anger returning.

"Keep it down man, she's exhausted. I don't wanna wake her," I tell him, trying to keep my own emotions in check.

"Sorry bro," he says, raking his hand through his hair once more.

"Do you wanna talk, son?" my uncle asks JP. JP shakes his head and closes his eyes.

"I'm gonna try to get some sleep," he says, turning his back to us and dragging his feet to his room. Once he shuts his door, my uncle turns to me.

"Tate are you okay? I know this situation must be hard for you," he says, and I shrug my shoulders, not knowing how to answer. My aunty steps to me, wrapping her small arms around me. Making me think of my mum, I squeeze her to me for a minute before I let go.

"I might try to get some sleep too. It's been a long night," I tell them, and they nod in unison, probably feeling the same way. "Night," I call out, as I turn my back to them. My feet lead me back to where my heart lies, next to my broken girl.

"Night," I hear them both say behind me, as I close the door. I step carefully towards the bed in the dark, pull the covers back and hop in. I reach out for Tamsyn and in her sleep she moves back into my chest, clinging to me. I hold her close, slipping my hand under my t-shirt she's wearing, needing her warm skin to soothe me. Resting my hand against her lower back, I wait for sleep to take me as well.

Movement from my side pulls me from my sleep. My mind catches up and I realise it's Tamsyn. She's sitting up, drawing in deep breaths. I sit up and put my arm around her shoulder.

"Hey," is all I say, trying not to scare her. I'm all too familiar with her reaction. She's had a nightmare. Her wide eyes find mine in the dark. A small amount of light peeks in through the window to show our faces to each other. I cup her face and she breaks down, tears streaming down again. I move my back against the wall and pull her onto my lap. Holding her to me, I let her cry all the pain out until they soften.

"Do you wanna talk about it?" I quietly ask. She doesn't respond for a few minutes and I take that as a no but then she starts talking.

"He rang me and started talking about the dock and I was so confused. It wasn't until he started talking about being free that I clicked. I was so scared. I ran all the way to the dock." She's quiet, collecting her thoughts before she continues. I rub my hand up and down her back, letting her know I'm here for her. With a shaky voice she says, "He was face down in the water when I got there. I didn't think, I just jumped in. I struggled to drag him to shore but he wasn't breathing," her voice cracks, so I squeeze her to me. I can't imagine what she went through. Rafe is bigger than me and Tamsyn is tiny compared to me. I hate to think of what she went through to save him. The amount of strength she would have needed to get him out of the water alone would have been huge. My broken girl has come so far, she's so strong.

I don't speak, not knowing what to say and wanting her to continue on her own. We sit in silence for a while before she says, "His eyes were blank Tate. It's as if everything that makes him Rafe was gone." The sobs unleash as I press her into me, trying to comfort her but not knowing if I'm making a difference. We stay in this position until the first rays of the morning sun hit my window. Her breaths evened out a while ago but I couldn't bring myself to sleep, in case she needed me.

She rouses a while later, snuggling her face against my chest before she fully wakes. Blue, puffy eyes peer up at me. I lean forward to rest my lips on her forehead, closing my eyes. Squeezing her tightly, I hold her for a minute before we need to face the day. Listening to her forced inhale and exhale, I know she's trying to keep herself from crying.

"If you need to cry Sweetness, it's okay. You don't need to be strong in front of me," I tell her. I want her to be real with me, no matter whether that's with tears or smiles. She sniffles but no tears.

"Did JP and his parents come home?" she quietly asks, her voice sounding hoarse from the night of crying.

"Yeah, but Rafe wouldn't see them, so they didn't speak to him," I tell her. She glances back up to me with unshed tears shimmering on her lower lash line. I deliver another chaste kiss to her forehead not knowing what else to say. "You hungry?" I try directing ourselves in a different direction.

"No, not really," she says, resting her head against my chest.

"What about coffee? I could use one," I say. I'm probably going to need more than one to have enough energy to get through today. She nods against my chest so I lift her off me and shuffle out of bed. Holding my hand out to her, she clasps it and I pull her to stand. We walk hand in hand down the hallway. We are about to pass the bathroom but she squeezes my hand.

"I'm gonna use the bathroom," she says.

"Okay, I'll meet you in the kitchen. It's just down the hall," I tell her. She looks at the floor before her eyes raise to mine.

"Umm, can I use your toothbrush?" she whispers, and I can't help but beam at her because even in this broken moment, she looks adorable.

"Sure," I say, pulling her into the bathroom and pulling my blue toothbrush from the holder on the sink, laying it down for her. I kiss her temple, leave her and walk into the kitchen where I'm greeted by JP and his parents. JP doesn't look my way, his eyes focused on the kitchen table where he sits.

"Morning Tate," my aunty says, and I offer her a small smile. "Is Tamsyn still sleeping?" she asks.

"No, she's using the bathroom. She's not very hungry so I'm just gonna make some coffee," I inform her, moving over to the kettle and filling it with water. Placing it back on it's holder, I press the button down to boil the water. Grabbing the milk from the fridge along with two mugs, I place them on the bench waiting for Tamsyn to join us as I don't know how she likes hers. As she steps into the kitchen all eyes fling to her, even JP. "How do you like your coffee?" I ask her quietly, as she steps into my side. She takes the teaspoon I offer her. She scoops two spoonfuls of coffee and then another two of sugar, plus milk. I commit it to memory so I'll know for future use. The landline phone rings, everyone's eyes directed to it. My aunt gets up to answer it.

"Hello?" she says into the receiver, then her eyes glance up to Tamsyn. "Sure, Tanya, she's right here," she says, before holding the phone out to Tamsyn. "It's your mum, honey," she softly says, smiling at Tamsyn. Tamsyn steps quickly to the phone, grasping it in two hands to her ear.

"Hi Mum," she says. She's quiet for a beat while her mum must be talking. Her brows furrow in confusion, then I see the tears start to form so I move towards her.

"What is it?" I ask, and she shakes her head.

"Mum tried ringing my phone and was worried. I forgot I dropped it on the dock," she whispers, as I wipe a tear off her cheek. She listens to her mum talk some more before she says ,"Okay, I'll see you later then Mum," before she hangs up and looks up at me. "I can stay with you today, can't I?" she hesitantly asks.

"Of course" I tell her, a small smile ghosting my lips. We grab the coffees I finished making and take seats at the table with the others. JP pushes his chair back roughly.

"I'm gonna go for a walk. I'll be back soon," he says, before he leaves quickly. My aunt and uncle exchange a look between them while they sip their own coffees. Silence fills the air, everyone simmering with their own thoughts.

14

"Do you think Rafe would be up to having visitors today?" I ask my aunt.

"I'm not sure. I can give his mum a ring today if you like and see how he's doing," she says. I nod in reply. "Why don't you two try to catch up on some sleep this morning. I'll let you know if I hear anything," my aunty suggests. I look to Tamsyn and she gives a slight nod which my aunty catches. They finish off their drinks and place them in the sink, leaving without saying much else. Tamsyn and I sit there sipping our drinks until we finish ourselves.

"I'll meet you in the room Sweetness? I'm gonna use the bathroom," I tell her, and she nods as I take her cup for her. I watch her from the sink as she shuffles her feet towards my room. I wash the cups, placing them on the tray to drain then enter the bathroom. After relieving myself I brush my teeth, highly aware of the fact Tamsyn used it before me. Weirdly it has me smiling to myself. Using the same toothbrush is quite intimate.

I finish up and walk to my room. Entering, my breath catches at the sight of Tamsyn curled up under the blankets in a ball. She looks so tiny. I close the door and climb in beside her, drawing her to my chest. She wiggles her delicate hand up and under my shirt, resting it on my chest where my heartbeat would be felt. I don't question her, giving her whatever she needs at this time to keep her held together. Her warmth seeps into me and lack of sleep from last night has my eyes drooping. No counting sheep needed, sleep comes swiftly.

Don't Fade. Breathe Easy.

Chapter 3

-- Tamsyn --

The squeak of the door opening, has my eyes opening from the light sleep I managed to fall into. I quickly slip my hand out from under Tate's shirt, trying not to wake him but failing. He stirs, rubbing his eyes, directing his focus my way. JP creeps in past the door and holds out his hand. I reach out my own shaking hand, taking my phone from his grip.

"How?" I ask, in shock.

"I went down to the dock and it was sitting on the edge in the corner. It's probably ruined because of the rain last night, but thought you might like it back anyway," he sadly says.

"Thanks," I say.

"Yeah, thanks man," Tate adds. "You okay?" he asks him.

"Not sure. I just wanna see him, you know," JP says, his gaze directed at the floor.

"Shit! JP, can you contact Penny and Scott to let them know," I say. They'd completely slipped my mind.

"Already done. I rang them both and filled them in. Think they might pop around later," he states. I follow his sad voice and gaze at him. Pain clearly etched in his features. He lingers by the door and I wish I could ease his hurt.

"JP, why don't you come sit down with us for a bit?" I suggest, trying to offer him some comfort. He stares at me before glancing at Tate who nods at him, encouraging him. He slowly drags his feet forward so I pat the other side of the bed by me. He comes over and leans his back on the wall, sitting on top of the covers. I'm squished between both of them now so I take one of each of their hands in mine, hoping we can keep each other strong.

Time passes with us clutching each other's hands and it isn't until JP's dad pops his head in the door that we release.

"You guys have a couple of visitors," he tells us, looking at JP.

"Send them in," Tate says, beside me. Not a minute later, Scott and Penny traipse through Tate's door. Both of their eyes are red, Penny's from crying and Scott's from holding tears back but not very successfully. As soon as Penny catches sight of us, the tears fall freely from both our eyes. I shuffle over the duvet and into her embrace.

"Aww Tam," she whispers between her sniffles, squeezing me harder. I release her and swipe roughly against the devastation on my cheeks. I give Penny a little side nod to indicate she should go to JP. He needs her more at the moment. She catches on and crawls before him, his eyes stay firmly on the blanket. I watch out of the corner of my eye as she slides a finger under his chin, raising his eyes to hers. It's like her gaze makes JP crack and his heartbreak gets released. Tears flood down his face as he pulls Penny into his chest, holding her tight. If it wasn't for such a heartbreaking occasion, I would be swooning over how cute they are. Tate, Scott and I try to be discreet and leave them but JP catches our exit.

"No, stay guys. It's fine," he says, still clinging to Penny. We all move back to our places. Scott takes a spot at the foot of the bed.

We're all silent for a while until Scott asks, "Does anyone know if he's up for visitors?"

The three of us shake our heads and then JP says, "He refused to see me last night so I'm not sure if it'll be the same story today or not." A jolt shoots through me as I realise I'm still in Tate's baggy clothes without any underwear, surrounded by my friends.

It makes me self conscious so I lean up to whisper in Tate's ear, "Hey, could you take me home to change my clothes please?" His eyes scan my body and I see a flicker of heat behind his eyes before a small smile graces his lips and he kisses my forehead.

"Sure," he whispers to me, then he says to JP, "Bro, can I borrow your car please? Just gonna take Tamsyn to get some clothes." JP looks over to me. No one realised I was in Tate's clothes and it was just my stupid head.

He digs in his pockets, pulling the keys out and handing them over to Tate before asking, "You cool if we just hang in here?"

"Yeah man, no problem. We won't be long," Tate says, before turning to me. "Come on, let's go." I shuffle off the bed, taking my damaged phone with me. I don't even have shoes. Tate leaves me in the hall for a minute while he disappears into the bathroom and then emerges with a plastic bag, handing it to me. "Your clothes. I didn't have time to wash them," he says, and I lean my head back, giving him a small smile.

"That's okay. I'll chuck them in the machine when I get home," I tell him, then we head out to JP's car. "What's the time?" I ask, having no idea how much of the day has passed.

Tate turns the car on and the clock appears on the dashboard as he says, "Looks like it's one o'clock. Half the day has disappeared."

We pull up outside my house and get out of the car. Tate comes around and grasps my hand in his. He does his signature move, running his thumb back and forth across my hand, comforting me. As we step through the front door, my mum must hear us as she comes from the kitchen to greet us.

She wraps me in a hug and then surprisingly does the same with Tate.

"How are you two holding up?" she asks, peering into both our eyes, looking for the answer there.

"We're okay Mum," I tell her. "We came home so I could change my clothes." She looks at me, nodding. "I'm gonna put these in the machine. I'll meet you in my room, Tate," I tell him over my shoulder, as I move to the laundry. I flip open the washing machine lid and shake the contents of my bag out into it. Mum comes in behind me and takes the washing powder from my hands.

"I'll take care of this bub." She places the powder down on the bench, grasping both my hands and turning me her way. "Now, how are you really feeling?" she queries, and the unwanted tears fall as she pulls me into a hug.

"I need to see him for myself. I need to see he's okay with my own eyes. It's like I can't fully catch my breath until I see he's alright. My mind still thinks he's in the same condition he was when the ambulance took him away and it's going into overdrive with worry," I admit into her shoulder.

"I'm sure you'll get to see him soon enough honey," she says, rubbing my back. After a minute I step out of her embrace but she clings to my hands again. "Now I know you lost your phone last night so I went out this morning and grabbed you a new one. It's in your room charging. It's probably ready now," she tells me, as she smiles and I offer a small one in return.

"Thanks Mum," I tell her, giving her another small hug before I make my way upstairs to my room. As I enter, I take in the view for a second, Tate lying down on my bed flicking through the channels on the T.V mindlessly. My movement catches his eye and his perfect smile shines my way as he pats the bed. I climb on the bed and cuddle on his chest, listening to the beating of his heart. I do it subconsciously as if my own heart needs to hear his beating away in his chest to know he's okay. He runs his strong fingers through my hair and I take a minute to breathe and pull myself together. I glance up at his face as he looks at me and cups my face. My body ignites on fire from his gaze, the magnet that has always pulled us together, draws my lips to his. His hand moves, caressing my face gently but I'm desperate for him, for the feeling he fills me with so I tug his head closer to me. He senses the shift in me and opens his mouth, gaining access to mine. He rolls me over onto my back as we get lost in each other, kissing like we can't breathe without the other. He holds his weight off me with his forearm by my head. A few minutes later, he pulls away looking down at me, gazing into my eyes, both of us catching our breaths. He slowly leans forward, pressing a lingering kiss first to my swollen lips and then another to my forehead before he hastily rolls off, pulling me back to rest my head on his chest. Only a few seconds later and my mum is knocking on my open door. Did he hear her and know she was coming? My mum had completely slipped my mind. I was so lost in Tate, I couldn't think.

"What do you think of your phone bub?" Mum asks, and I'd forgotten to even look for it. Once I'd seen Tate in my bed, everything else had faded away into the background.

"Sorry Mum, where did you put it?" I ask, sitting up on my bed. She walks over to the dresser where she's plugged it in and brings it over to me, placing it in my hand. It's the latest Samsung and she's even gotten me a silver glitter cover for it.

"Thanks so much Mum, this is awesome," I tell her, gratefully.

"No worries honey," she says as she exits the room. I sit with my legs crossed on the bed, turning it on.

"You should be able to sync all of your old phone content to this one with your Google account, I think," Tate says, sitting up next to me. We manage to sort out how to sync it and set it aside to finish while I hunt through my drawers for some clothes to change into.

"I'm going to have a shower," I tell him, my cheeks heating as I think about my last shower where we got a bit carried away. He must notice the blush as he gives me a knowing smile, his mind going to the same place as mine. I force myself to walk out of the room and into the bathroom before I jump back into his arms.

Once I'm showered and in my own t-shirt and sweatpants, I carry his with me back to the room.

"I'll put your clothes in a bag so you can take them home," I tell him.

"Or you could leave them here, just in case I need them sometime," he says shyly, focusing on the T.V. like what he said isn't a big deal. I don't say anything, moving towards my dresser and placing the clothes on top. I get dragged from my thoughts by the ringing of Tate's phone. He pulls it out of his pocket, looking at the screen. "It's JP," he tells me, as he answers. "Hey man," he says, listening to what JP has to say. "Sweet man, see you there," he says, hanging up.

Turning his gaze to me he says, "JP and the others are heading to the hospital in Penny's car. Rafe's mum rang and talked to my aunty and she wanted us to all go up and see him."

I can feel my hands tremble but I manage to keep my voice even as I say, "What are we waiting for? Let's go." I grab my new phone and put it in my pocket as we step down the stairs, finding my mum in the lounge. "We're heading to the hospital to see Rafe," I tell her, and her sad eyes find mine as she nods.

"Okay bub, ring me if you need me." I return her nod, grabbing Tate's hand as we leave the house and walk quietly to the car.

Don't Fade. Breathe Easy.

Chapter 4

-- Tate --

We arrive at the hospital and quietly wander through the corridors grasping onto each other's hand tightly. The disinfectant smell reminds me of my time spent in the hospital next to Quinn's bed. I force myself to push those thoughts away. I need to be present in this moment and be strong for Tamsyn. I can feel the slight tremble of her hand that she thinks she's hiding from me. I hate to think what must be going through her head, having found Rafe and saving him.

As we approach the door, we stop outside both needing to take a breath before entering. Pushing the door open, JP's harsh voice hits us.

"You're obviously not okay. What do you have to be sad about anyway?" He is practically yelling and I know exactly who he's directing it at. We round the curtain and see JP hovering over Rafe who is lying in bed, a white sheet draped over his body. Penny and Scott stand against the far wall.

"I'm fine. It was an accident man, I've already told you that. I slipped," Rafe says, trying to use his charm to convince them, not having noticed me and Tamsyn yet. Tamysn's breath catches, I'm not sure whether it's from Rafe's words or seeing him for the first time after the incident. It draws everyone's eyes our way. I keep my focus on Rafe's face, wanting to see his reaction to her. His face drops, the charm washing away as he takes in the trembling girl next to me who saved his life. I don't need to look at her to know tears are rushing down her cheeks. I can feel the sight of Rafe in the hospital bed has Tamsyn's heart silently breaking for him. I squeeze her hand, sending her comfort to let her know I'm here.

"Shit," he utters, as he sees the devastation wash over her at what his actions have caused. Their gazes stay locked on each other. He opens his arms to her but she takes a step closer to me. Rafe notices the slight movement, his hands dropping to his side. He closes his eyes and I watch as he takes in a shaky breath. When his eyes open again they're coated with a wetness I've never seen on Rafe's face before. He's always been a smiling presence in any situation. I feel the tug on my hand so release Tamsyn's hand knowing she can't resist going to him now. She scurries to his side and jumps into his bed where he holds her tightly to him. The floodgates burst and she loudly sobs into his chest. It hurts me to watch him comfort her when I want to be the one who offers her comfort. I know it's a selfish feeling so I force myself to push those feelings aside because this is what she needs and only Rafe can give this to her.

"Come on guys, how about we give them a minute?" I suggest to the others, and they look at me then follow me out of the door.

As we are leaving I hear Rafe's shaky voice saying, "Petal, it's okay," before the door closing blocks their voices from our ears. Out in the corridor JP's anger returns as he paces back and forth.

"JP, you alright man?" I ask, knowing he is anything but okay.

"He's trying to convince everyone it was an accident. Like it wasn't supposed to happen," he says, the frustration in his voice leaking out of him. "How are we supposed to help him if he doesn't even acknowledge there's a problem?"

"Just be there for him man," I say to him, squeezing his shoulder.

His shattered gaze shifts to mine as he says, "I'm his best friend. Why wouldn't he tell me what was going on? I, of all people, should have realised something wasn't right but I had no idea." His voice cracks at the end so I draw him into me for a hug. I know exactly how he feels. I was Quinn's twin and I had no idea what was going on with her.

I hold him for a minute before releasing him and saying, "If he didn't want you to know, you wouldn't have seen it. They're good at hiding it." His eyes twitch in response as he realises I'm talking about Quinn too.

"You alright?" he asks me, and I nod, knowing what he's referring to without mentioning her name. Penny comes up beside him, taking his hand in hers which directs his attention to her which I'm thankful for. I don't want to think about Quinn right now. I'd rather we focus on Rafe. I can let Quinn consume my thoughts later but for now, I need to stay clear headed for Rafe and Tamsyn. I push my back against the wall and slide down until I'm sitting next to Scott who has taken a spot on the floor.

"You think he'll be okay?" Scott sadly asks, focussing on a random spot on the opposite wall.

"I really hope so," I say, as my head drops forward. We all let the silence surround us as we wait. After about ten minutes of waiting patiently, Rafe's parents arrive and greet JP.

"Hi son, you alright?" Rafe's dad asks JP, and he nods in answer. Rafe is the splitting image of his dad. His mum's slender frame is shaking as she gazes at JP, her worry for her son dripping off her.

"He said it was an accident," his mum says to JP, but the way she says it, you can hear the doubt in her voice. JP stares at her for a beat before he takes her hand in his.

"It wasn't an accident. He rang our friend Tamsyn before it happened. She said he was talking weird but she's sure it wasn't an accident," he informs them both. Rafe's mum's hand covers her mouth as her own tears spring to her eyes. Her husband pulls her into his side. "Talk to Tamsyn when you get a chance. She's in there with him now," he informs them.

"She's the one who saved him?" Rafe's dad asks.

"He rang her before it happened and she ran all the way there, called emergency services and pulled him out of the water and gave him CPR," I tell everyone, letting them know exactly what my girl went through last night. She's going to need more than me to get her through what she experienced. Penny's sniffles bring my gaze to her and I see the tears clogging her eyes. Her love for Tamsyn is obvious when she's thinking of what Tamsyn must be feeling right now. It makes me appreciate Tamsyn has a friend like her around. She's needed a girl to have her back fully.

"What are you guys doing out here?" Rafe's dad asks.

"We were giving Rafe and Tamsyn some space to talk," JP tells him. He nods in reply as he keeps his wife tucked into his side, comforting her.

"Do you kids want a hot drink or anything?" his dad asks.

"No thanks," we all surprisingly reply in unison.

"Well, we might give Rafe a bit longer with Tamsyn while we go get a coffee. We'll be back in a bit," he says to no one in particular. Rafe's parents turn on their heels and make their way back down the corridor which they came from. The rest of us retreat back into our heads, the silence surrounding us once again while we wait. My mind wanders to Tamsyn and hopes she's all right.

Chapter 5

-- Tamsyn --

"I'm fine. It was an accident man, I've already told you that. I slipped," Rafe says to JP, trying to convince him. I can't control my shaking. I'm not sure why all eyes are suddenly on me, I'm focussed on the helpless boy stretched out on the hospital bed. He lifts his arms up for me but staring at him, I don't believe the smile on his face so my body won't let me go to him. Instead my body automatically takes a step towards Tate, needing his strength. Rafe's face releases the smile he was faking and I see the hurt laced across it which he usually hides. As he closes his eyes, I draw in a breath. He's not faking anymore. The river of tears fall from his eyes and I race to him. I jump into his embrace, pressing my ear to his chest to hear his heartbeat, to reassure me it's not a dream. He's here. He's safe. His embrace around me is just as tight as mine. I hear Tate's voice but I can't focus on the words while the thumping in my ear calms me.

"Petal, it's okay," Rafe says, and I sob because it's anything but okay. How could this boy, who is a ray of light, be so miserable inside?

"It's not okay, Rafe. You're not okay," I mumble into his chest. His fist goes under my chin moving my eyes up to meet his watery gaze.

"I'm okay, I promise," he says. "It was an accident," he tells me, which has my blood boiling.

"Don't Rafe. You can lie to everyone else but not me. Please don't lie to me. You were talking about being free," I plead with him. He closes his eyes to compose himself before responding.

"It was the alcohol talking. I slipped. You gotta believe me," he begs. I don't understand why he's trying to act like everything is fine.

"Do you know what happened?" I ask him.

"I vaguely remember calling you then I slipped and fell into the water and someone pulled me out and gave me CPR. My parents didn't tell me much else and my memory isn't very good because of the alcohol," he says. My breath catches because he doesn't know it was me who saved him. I leap out of the bed, tears streaming uncontrollably down my face. "What is it?" he asks. With a shaky voice I fill him in on the details he doesn't know.

"It was me. I saved you," I tell him, staring straight into his devastated face.

"Petal, I'm sor...,"

"Don't," I cut him off. "I raced down to the dock and you were face down in the water. I jumped in and I had to drag you to shore." I take a breath as I'm puffing, getting worked up explaining what happened. He lowers his eyes but he has to face this. "Look at me," I all but scream at him. I gesture to my small frame running my hand up and down. "I had to drag your massive body out of the water and all I could think was please let me have the strength to do this while begging for you to be okay. You weren't breathing when I got you to shore so I had to give you CPR," I tell him. His eyes plead with me to believe it was an accident, but all it does is make my skin burn with anger. "You weren't fucken breathing Rafe. Do you get that? Do you get how not okay that is?" The weight of the night before pulls me to my knees as I fall apart. I cover my face with my hands as I crumble. Strong arms engulf me and pull me up into a firm chest carrying me back to his bed.

"Don't cry Petal. I'm okay. I'm still here," he whispers, and I cry harder because he's still trying to convince me. Why can't he let the lie go already? He cradles my head against his chest and that's how we remain until we hear the door opening. Rafe's arms stiffen around me and it's quiet for a minute until I hear Tate's voice.

"Tamsyn, you alright?" he asks, the concern evident in his voice. I disengage myself from Rafe and hurry to Tate who lifts me up into his arms, my legs and arms squeezing the life out of him as I shake with anger and hurt. I know Rafe's hurting but I'm hurting too. Rafe denying anything is wrong is just making it worse. How can we help him if he won't admit it? "Do you wanna go?" Tate whispers in my ear, and I nod my head against his neck.

"Tamsyn, please don't leave like this," Rafe begs, which has me looking up at him through my tear stained eyes.

I keep my voice steady as I say in front of everyone, his parents included, "You can lie to everyone Rafe but not me. I know the truth. You need help. No one is going to think any less of you. Just ask for it. You're not okay and you won't be until you can admit it wasn't an accident and you need help." All my strength has left my body and Tate carries me out of the room, not letting me down until we get to JP's car.

"What happened Sweetness? You're shaking," he says, as he helps me into the passenger seat. I feel the chill at the loss of his body contact and tears still drip down my face. He hops into the driver's seat and takes my hand in his, making my eyes find his. Worry covers all his features.

"Rafe is trying to convince everyone it was an accident and it's making me so mad. It wasn't an accident. You believe me, don't you?" I ask, as I start to wonder if I've gotten it wrong myself. No, I'm a hundred percent sure it wasn't an accident.

"Of course I do. From what you told me Rafe said on the phone, it doesn't sound like he was in a good headspace last night," he gently says. I let the conversation with Rafe from the night before run through my head, coming to the same conclusion; it wasn't an accident.

"Why won't he ask for help and admit something is wrong?" I ask. Tate releases my hand and cups my face, brushing my tears away with his thumb.

"We know more than anyone how hard it is to ask for help, Sweetness. All we can do is be there for him and let him know we are here when he's ready. We can't force him to ask for help," he softly says. I know Tate's words make sense because I never reached out and asked for help. If it hadn't been for Tate noticing me, I would probably still be walking around in a perpetual haze of grief.

"That doesn't feel like it's enough though. What if he tries something again?" My words crack as a sob escapes, thinking of what could have happened last night if I hadn't gotten there in time. What if I couldn't save him? Tate's arms surround me as he hugs me awkwardly over the center console. He embraces me until my sobs quieten down then releases me.

"How about we go back to your place and watch some T.V?" He asks, starting the car.

"Sure," I say, needing to lie down and do nothing else for the rest of the day. Silence fills the car as Tate drives us to my house.

As we enter my house, my mum rushes to us and asks, "How is he?" She sounds as worried about Rafe as we are.

"He's acting like it was an accident and that there's nothing wrong with him," I tell her. I can hear my anger rearing its head again.

"Give him time bub," she says.

"We're gonna go watch some Netflix," I tell her, as I turn to walk up the stairs with Tate at my back. I kick my shoes off, grab my remote off the bedside table, turn the T.V. on and start flicking through movies.

Tate takes his own shoes off and sits next to me, pulling me into his chest and kissing my temple. I click on the first movie, not caring what it is and snuggle into Tate's warm embrace. I close my eyes, letting the exhaustion I still feel wash over me, dragging me into slumber.

-- Tate --

My fingers run through her soft hair, as her gentle snores fill the room. I haven't been able to focus on the movie knowing she's hurting and I don't know what to do about it. I get why Rafe is denying it. When you are trapped in a darkness so neverending it's as if there's no way out. The voices in your head twist your thoughts and convince you that no one wants to hear about your problems. That no one will help you if you say anything. That you are a burden. That you aren't worthy of help. The voices tell you that what is going on in your head is normal and it's nothing to worry about until it gets to a point where you are so overwhelmed inside, fighting this inner battle that you explode. The darkness tried to convince me that I needed it to survive, that it was helping me but in reality it was cutting me off from everyone. The darkness eats away at you from the inside out until you are nothing but a shell, feeling trapped inside yourself with no way out. I couldn't help Quinn but maybe I can help Rafe before it's too late.

I peel my arm away from Tamsyn, moving her head to lay on the pillow. She stirs, her eyes peeking open at me. "Hey, go back to sleep. I'm gonna take JP's car back home and then I'll come back later," I say, and she sleepily nods, closing her eyes and drifting back to sleep. I hurry down the stairs and don't see Tanya anywhere so leave without saying goodbye. When I'm in JP's car I send him a text.

Tate: Hey man, you home yet?

I drum my fingers on the steering wheel, waiting for his reply.

JP: Yeah bro. Penny and Scott just left. Where are you?

Tate: With Tamsyn. I'll be home soon.

I throw my phone into the passenger seat as I drive in the direction of where I need to go.

Walking through the hospital corridors again, the smell fills my nose. I dread hospitals. It wasn't this bad when I had Tamsyn beside me keeping it at a distance but now walking the halls alone, it overwhelms me and reminds me of Quinn. I speed my steps up wanting to get away from the sanitary smell but not sure it's possible in this place. As I arrive at the corridor leading to Rafe's room I slow down, unsure if his parents are still here. For what I have to say, I want to be alone with Rafe. I inch towards the door and peer through the window but the curtain shields Rafe from view. I can't see his parents anywhere so I bite the bullet and push the door open and step inside.

Rafe's still in the same position lying down on his bed, headphones connected to his phone while his eyes are closed, listening to music. He's unaware of my presence so I take the empty seat beside his bed and nudge his forearm to get his attention. He jerks up from the shock of my touch until his eyes find me. Eyes I now notice contain an exhausted shine to them. Not a tired exhaustion but a tired of life exhaustion. He kept it hidden so well no one noticed until it was too late and he took drastic action. That's the problem.

"Hey man," I say, as he rolls his headphones around his phone, placing it on the cabinet beside his bed.

"Hey, I didn't think I'd see you again today," he softly says.

"Where are your parents?" I ask, knowing I need to say what I came for without anyone interrupting us.

"They've gone home. They've been here since last night so I shooed them away to rest," he tells me, as he wriggles back in his bed, getting comfortable. I can't help but stare at my bigger than life friend and wonder how long he's been dealing with this. "How's Tamsyn?" he asks.

I let out a sigh before saying, "She's sleeping at the moment. She doesn't know I'm here."

"So out with it, I know you didn't come here for warm and fluffies," he says, as if he's expecting a lecture. How many has he gotten today I wonder?

"Can I tell you something without you taking offence? Just listen please?" I ask him. His brows pinch as he nods. I lean back in my chair, stretching my legs out in front of me, one ankle crossed over the other as I clasp my hands together in my lap. I stare out Rafe's window, not sure I can say all this while looking at his face. I take a deep breath and start telling Rafe my story.

"You remember the day in the cafeteria when I fell apart?" I don't wait for his answer. I continue on like he's answered me. "I don't know how much of my story you know so I'll tell you it all. My dad had just uttered the words, 'Quinn died,' and in a second my world shattered. You saw me and I hate to think what I looked like but my body gave out. It stopped functioning how I needed it to. My mind shut down, it was trying to protect me from what I can tell you is the worst thing to happen in my life so far." I take a deep breath, steadying myself before continuing.

"You see, a few months prior to the day in the cafeteria, Quinn committed suicide." I close my eyes, accepting the fact but never having said it out loud before. "What she did changed my life. If she hadn't done what she did, I wouldn't have come here. I would be content and happy, without a care in the world. What she did, forced me to grow up. Typical teenage things seem so trivial to me now. Drama and gossip I want no part of because what use is it when my sister, my twin is dead? How can anything matter when she's not here to see any of it?" I glance his way, and he's listening intently, watching me.

"When I returned home after she died, I kept myself numb. I welcomed the darkness creeping over me and I spent most of my days curled up in bed staring at the ceiling. I couldn't function. I didn't know how to and I didn't want to without her. She took a part of my heart with her and I can't get it back. It was ripped out of my chest so violently with the shock of her death, I think my heart is going to be permanently damaged." I run a hand through my hair as I find the words to say next. "Everyone in our home town was affected. I wasn't very coherent at her funeral but I do know there were so many people around, paying their respects. Her friends were affected, her teachers, even the principal. My friends were a mess because of her death too. I had kids at school who've never talked to me before, look at me with pity or sadness because of Quinn. Her death has changed my parents. I don't think they'll ever be the same. No parent should ever have to bury their child. But losing a child to suicide leaves a momentous scar. She's impacted my life in more ways than she probably thought she ever would. She's affected Tamsyn because of me. And you know what? There are many more people out there she affected that I probably don't know, people that she came into contact with or made an impression on. There are bound to be guys who had crushes on her, my friend being one."

"She sent waves through more people's lives than she thought she would. She thought she was alone, but that was the complete opposite. I will forever live with the guilt of not seeing the signs that something wasn't right with her. How could I not, she was my twin. I should have been able to see it. I should have known something was wrong, shouldn't I?" I ask, defeat looking at him as he stares back at me.

"If she didn't want you to know man, there's no way you could have," he softly says, trying to ease my guilt but I see the truth in his words. He's saying them from his perspective.

"Put Tamsyn in my position and you in Quinn's. That is how our girl is feeling," I say. I call her 'our girl' because I see now, she belongs to all of us in different ways. He tries to shake his head. "She's a wreck man. Can you imagine what she went through last night, finding you?" He hangs his head, his own guilt eating at him. I give him a minute before I press harder. "Now imagine if she had been too late. If you weren't sitting in this hospital bed and we were getting ready to bury you instead, how do you think she would feel? Do you think she could survive losing someone else, especially when, if for a few minutes, she could have saved you?" His eyes lift to mine and I see the tears he's trying to hold in, his hands shaking. "I'm not trying to guilt you man, I just want you to see how losing you would have affected us all. I'd have to bury someone else I hold dear to me because of suicide. JP would have to bury his best friend man. Scott and Penny would lose a close friend too." The tears fall down his cheeks and he swipes angrily at them as if they've betrayed him.

His voice shakes as he finds the words, "I don't know why I feel like this. JP is right, I don't have a reason to feel sad and empty." I take his hand in mine.

"Hey, listen to me. Your thoughts are yours and yours alone. You have a right to feel exactly how you feel. It doesn't matter what other people say. They aren't in your head. Only you know what goes on in there. Sometimes there is no reason why you're feeling a certain way man. It could be a chemical imbalance causing it. But you need help. We need you to admit you need help, that you can't cope with this alone anymore man. Asking for help is the first step. It doesn't make you weak asking for help either, it makes you incredibly strong. We are all here for you, you've gotta take the first step though." He stares at me with his tear stained face, taking my words in. "Reaching out to someone and getting help is letting the light in. You've gotta let the light in to defeat the darkness. That's what I had to do," I tell him, hoping my words are getting through to him. He finally cracks, his body shudders with his pain as the tears begin to rain down his face. I stand up and pull his head to my chest, cradling him in a hug while this usually bubbly, full of life guy falls apart. I let him cry, letting out all the pain inside.

"I need help," he whispers, and I close my eyes in relief, glad I've gotten through to him.

"I know man and that's okay," I tell him gently, hoping he understands how okay it is to ask for help. Why is it so hard to ask for help when you're not coping?

"Who did you reach out to?" he softly asks, knowing I've fought my own battle with the darkness you can't see but feels so tangible.

"My little star of course, Tamsyn. I thought it would have been obvious," I say with a light chuckle.

He wipes his face before he says, "It makes sense I called her that night. Maybe in my own way, I was reaching out to her too."

"I'm glad you did man," I tell him honestly. I hate to think of a world where Rafe's smiling face isn't a part of it. I cling to him a bit longer before I say, "How about you ring your parents man? I know it'll be hard but I'm here." I can feel his anxiety wafting off of him but he picks up his phone and dials a number while I take my seat in the chair again.

"Hi Mum," his shaky voice says, after a few seconds. I don't know what she's saying but he's silent until he takes a big breath and looks at me as if he's talking to me. Maybe it makes it easier for his words to flow. "I'm not okay Mum. It wasn't an accident," his voice cracks at the end, the tears starting up again. I grab his hand for support as he listens to his mum's words. He answers whatever she's saying and then finishes with, "I love you too," before hanging up. Looking at me he says, "They're coming straight in."

"Do you want me to stay with you until they arrive?" I ask, and he nods, lying back on his bed releasing my hand. I get comfortable in the chair and we sit silently waiting. "Things are gonna be okay, Rafe. You're gonna be okay," I tell him.

"Thanks dude," he softly says. We wait another twenty minutes until his parents come rushing into the room. His mum's eyes are all bloodshot from tears. His dad looks paler than he did when I saw him earlier.

"Rafe," his mum says, as she rushes to his side, wrapping him in her arms and his tears start back up again.

"I'll leave you guys to it," I tell them, standing, ready to make my escape.

"Thanks Tate," Rafe says, and I offer a small smile, thankful he's on his way to getting the help he needs.

I turn to leave but his dad stops my exit with a hand to my shoulder and says, "Thank you, for whatever you did. Thank you." I glance at his face and see his own unshed tears.

"I'm glad I could help. Hopefully he can get the help he needs now," I say, and to that, he nods, releasing my shoulder and I walk out of the room. Once clear of Rafe's room my own tears break free, all the emotions I'm feeling flood over me. Sadness, hurt, pain, grief, relief and hope. With hope in my heart, I leave the hospital happy. I got through to Rafe and pray it's enough to help save him from himself.

Don't Fade. Breathe Easy.

Chapter 6

-- Tate --

I walk through the front door and no one is around so I head straight to JP's door, knocking before I enter.

Peeking around as I enter, I say, "Hey man." He's sitting on his bed in the same position I found his best friend, headphones in, listening to music. I hold out his car keys to him as he tugs the headphones from his ears.

"Thanks man. How's Tamsyn?" he asks, his voice laced with worry.

"She's a mess. She was sleeping when I left but I came back to drop off your car. Could you drop me back after I have a shower?" I ask, wanting to get back to Tamsyn as soon as possible.

"Sure bro, no worries," he says, as I take a seat on the end of his bed.

I don't want to beat around the bush so I spit it out, "I went to see Rafe again. He's asked his parents for help. Admitted it wasn't an accident after all." I let my eyes find JP's shocked face while he processes what I said.

Wiping a hand down his face he says, "So he did try to end his life last night?" he asks, his voice shaking. I nod in reply. "Shit," he utters, closing his eyes before they fly open, anger blinding them. "I don't get it. What could make him want to do that? He's the fucken happiest person I know. His parents are great, everyone loves him. I just don't get it," he says, sounding frustrated.

"You don't need to understand it man. Depression isn't biased. It can hit anyone, even the ones you think are the happiest and most put together people. You don't really know what's going on inside someone's head or what demons they are battling," I tell him.

He releases a sigh, "I should've known. He's my best friend." Guilt drips off his words. I shake my head not wanting him to feel how I do.

"I should've known what was going on with Quinn. She was my twin, but the fact is I didn't. She kept it so well hidden there's no way we could have known because she didn't want us to know. It's the same with Rafe. He hides it behind jokes and laughs, you don't second guess if he's happy behind his smile. Why would you? Why would anyone question him when he seems so happy? Appearances can be deceiving man. The fact is he didn't want anyone to know. We can only be thankful he's going to hopefully get the help he needs now."

"How come you went back to see him? I'd have thought you wouldn't want to leave Tamysn's side," he asks.

"It was seeing her suffer that made up my mind about going to see him. I couldn't let her live with the fact she knew it wasn't an accident and he was pretending it was. It was eating her up inside and I could only see it getting worse. So I went there and explained what happened after Quinn died, and how many people her death affected. It was just a different angle that happened to work," I explain, not wanting JP to think he couldn't make his best friend see sense himself.

"Thanks for that bro. I honestly don't know what I'd do without him," he says, and I see the tears glazing over his vision.

"Just take it easy on him okay. I think it's hard for people that haven't experienced depression to understand it but just be there for him. That's all he needs. No judgement, just be the best friend that he loves," I tell him truthfully, because I know that if I hadn't suffered through my own darkness I wouldn't have a clue what other people are suffering. It's made me more aware and it seems like there are way more people out there fighting their own demons than I ever thought possible.

"I will man. How about you go take a shower so I can drop you to Tamsyn," he suggests, and I don't hesitate, giving him a small smile as I go to the bathroom. After I'm showered and changed I walk out of my room on my way to JP's and get stopped by my aunty.

"Are you headed out Tate?" she asks, looking me up and down.

"Yeah, I was going to go back to Tamsyn and stay the night. Is that okay?" I ask, knowing I've got school tomorrow.

"Yeah that's fine honey. Do you need tomorrow off? I think JP is going to stay home," she tells me.

"That would be good," I say, realising a day off might be a good thing to get all my thoughts together before trying to get back into school.

"You doing okay?" she asks, and I notice the worry on her face.

"Yeah I'm okay. I will let you know if I'm not," I promise, as I take a step towards her, delivering a kiss to her cheek. I know her and my mum talk all the time, so I know my mum is worried about me.

"Thanks Tate, you have a good night," she says, as she walks down the hall towards the kitchen. I knock on JP's door. He's in the same position I left him in.

"You ready?" he asks.

"Yeah, if you are," I say.

"Yeah, I'll just throw my shoes on." When he's ready, he leads me out to his car to take me to my girl.

-- Tamsyn --

My eyes peel open at the noticeable weight that lies down next to me, pulling me into their hard chest. I breathe in his earthy scent and instantly relax knowing it belongs to Tate. Twisting my face up I gaze into his eyes, taking in his wet hair. "How long have you been gone for?" I say between a yawn, covering my mouth with my hand.

"Not too long. Did you have a good sleep?" he asks.

"Yeah, I did actually. I've been out since you left," I admit, as I wriggle around so I'm lying with my chin on his chest so I can see him better. With a tiny smirk on his face he wiggles his hand under my top that's ridden up and draws small circles on my lower back with the lightest touch. I focus on the feel of his fingers on my skin and get lost in the sensation. It feels like something has shifted between us, our connection more electric since he returned for my birthday.

With his free hand, he runs it through his longer locks as he says, "So I went to see Rafe again.' I stiffen at his words but he continues on with his circle movements. "It's nothing bad, Sweetness, relax," he tells me, which has my body loosening but still unable to relax, until he tells me the whole story.

"Did something happen?" I ask.

He stares intensely into my eyes as he says, "I explained what I went through with Quinn dying and how that affected me and everyone around me." He continues his light movements as he closes his eyes for a beat then says, "I told him how my own darkness affected me and how

44

I had to reach out to someone before it started to get better." His words cause tears to drip down my face onto his t-shirt.

"Is he going to get help?" I ask, my voice shaky with hope.

"He called his parents Sweetness. He told them he needs help and that it wasn't an accident," he says, staring into my eyes. My whole body starts to shudder so he places his hands under my arms and hoists me flat against his chest, crushing me in a hug. "It's okay baby. He's gonna be okay now," he whispers into my ear. I maneuver my hands under his neck to squeeze him back as he holds me while I let all the tears fall, needing to release them all. All the pain and relief rolled into one big emotion. His large hand rubs up and down my back, letting me take my time to let it all out. A heavy wave of relief floods me as I know Rafe will get the help he needs. We stay wrapped in each other's embrace for a while as I let everything out. When my tears have finally run dry, I lift my head from where it was buried in his neck to stare into his eyes.

"Thank you for doing that," I tell him, grateful he came back into my life. He not only saved me but he has helped save Rafe too.

"It was no problem at all. I'm honestly just glad I got through to him," he says, and I catch his glance to my lips. I move the last bit of distance pressing my lips against his, closing my eyes. His arms around me tighten as he deepens the kiss. I press my body firmly against his and savour the moment.

"Ahem," I hear the fake cough coming from my door and I jump off Tate as if I've been shocked by an electric fence. My mum's amused face is staring back at us as I wipe my mouth with the back of my hand. "Definitely keep this door open," she says, and I'm mortified she walked in on us like that.

"I thought you might like to know Tanya, that Rafe has admitted to his parents that he needs help," Tate directs at Mum, thankfully changing the subject while I feel my face heat up.

"Awww, that's wonderful news," she says, with her own tears in her eyes. I know she cares about the guys as much as I do. They've become a permanent fixture in my life now and I know she's always had a soft spot for Rafe. A lot of people do. She flings a tear across her cheek, collecting herself before she says, "I just got off the phone with your aunty Tate, she said you were going to have tomorrow off school and wanted to double check it was okay for you to stay the night." I raise my eyes because I didn't know he was planning to stay but I'm excited at the prospect.

"Is that alright Mum?" I ask, hopeful.

"Yeah, that's fine bub. I told her I'd let you stay home tomorrow as well. It's been an emotional weekend." I think of Rafe and sadly nod at her. "Now, make sure you leave the door open," she warns firmly, but I see the amusement in her eyes. She knows how much I missed Tate when he was gone, so I know she's happy he's back for good. "I've made some chicken stir fry and there's enough for you Tate, if you two want to come down for dinner." I look to Tate and he nods. I'm starving and Tate's a growing boy who is always hungry so we shuffle off the bed and follow Mum downstairs.

Once Mum is a few steps ahead of us, I lean up on tippy toes and whisper sarcastically in his ear, "Well that wasn't embarrassing at all." His light chuckle draws my eyes to his and he delivers a small kiss to my forehead as we walk hand in hand down the stairs.

Chapter 7

-- Tate --

The next morning I'm pulled out of my sleep by my phone ringing where I left it on Tamsyn's bedside table. She stirs as I grab my phone, probably getting woken by the noise too. I glance at the caller ID and see it's JP.

I swipe to answer and say, "Hey man," as I wrap my arm tighter around Tamsyn's body that's tucked into my side.

"Hey, what are you and Tamsyn doing?" he asks.

"We were still sleeping, what time is it?" I question, thinking it was still early.

"It's nearly lunchtime," he informs me.

"Oh man, I guess we both needed to catch up on our sleep."

"Yeah, makes sense. I haven't had much sleep since the other night either," he says softly. "Anyway, I was ringing because Rafe's dad rang me. He wanted me to gather all Rafe's friends who were at the hospital yesterday together to head in today and see him for some reason. It's got me a bit anxious. I guess I'm always going to expect something bad now" he says, as his voice drops in volume.

"It won't always be like this man. He will hopefully get the help he needs to feel better."

"I really hope so," he sighs.

"What time did they want us at the hospital?" I ask, trying to distract him from his worrying. My question has Tamsyn lifting her head off my chest, inspecting my face for clues as to what's going on in my conversation.

"They just said as soon as we were ready to head in there. You were my first call. I'm going to ring Penny and Scott now. I think they were both taking the day off school as well. I'll text you after I talk to them but probably best to get ready so we can go as soon as possible."

"Sweet man, sounds like a plan. Talk soon."

"Laters," JP says, ending the call.

"What was that about?" Tamsyn asks, sitting up next to me on the bed, while I replace my phone on the bedside table.

"Rafe's dad wants us all to go to the hospital for some reason. So let's get up and get ready so we are ready when JP talks to Scott and Penny," I say, as I lean over and kiss her temple.

"Okay then, I might jump in the shower first," she says, as she scoots off the bed, walking to her dresser to grab some clothes. "I won't be too long," she says, with her clothes gathered in her arms as she leaves me lying in bed.

I lean back on the pillow and close my eyes, breathing deeply. All this stuff with Rafe is so overwhelming, I need a minute to just breathe. I focus on my inhale and exhale. Trying to remember what the hippy lady said at senior retreat we did earlier in the year. I let all the thoughts circle in my head and let them drift away, not holding them for long. My thoughts are mixed with images of Rafe's smiling face and ones of Quinn too. It still pains my heart to picture her but I hope one day it will get easier. I know my mum wants me to see someone in regards to Quinn and I'm starting to think it wouldn't be such a bad idea. I want to be someone Tamsyn can depend on so I need to fix my head. I can't always be struggling to stay and fight or ready to run whenever I think of my sister.

As my eyes are closed and I'm lost in my breathing, I sense Tamsyn walk into the room. I feel her as she inches closer to me and leans down, her soft lips pressing a kiss to the corner of my mouth.

"You look so peaceful," she whispers, with our lips touching. Her minty breath fills my lungs.

The minty smell has me sitting up and murmuring, "Can I use your toothbrush?" between pursed lips.

She leans back smirking at me saying, "Are you trying to hide your morning breath from me?" I shake my head vigorously, while trying not to laugh.

She lets out a soft chuckle saying, "My toothbrush is the red one in the bathroom." I throw the covers off and kiss her on the forehead while a smile lingers on her face as I rush to the bathroom. Bad breath seems so trivial to worry about with everything else going on but I still want my girl to want to kiss me. I hurriedly brush my teeth and get back to Tamsyn. She's strapping on her sandals as I enter. Her hair hanging loose in front of her as she leans over to fiddle with the buckle. As she straightens I can't help myself. I cup her face and press a kiss to her lips.

"I'm so lucky I found you," I whisper, which has her cheeks tingeing pink.

She wraps her arms around my neck and presses her body flush against mine, before replying, "I'm the lucky one." She leans in and deepens the kiss. I tug her closer, our minty breaths mixing together.

Lately I can't get enough of my girl whenever I'm near her. As we pull apart, both of our laboured breaths can be heard as we stare into each other's eyes. Our unspoken words drift between us. Both of us are feeling the electric charge that has surrounded us lately and it's only intensifying.

My phone ringing breaks our stare off so I turn to grab it, answering.

"Hey bro, we are ready now. I'll pick up Scott then come for you guys and Penny is going to meet us there. That good?" JP asks.

"Sweet man, we will wait outside," I tell him, and he hangs up. "Let's go," I say to Tamsyn, as I grab her hand and lead her to the stairs.

"Mum said she was needed in the office early this morning so would've already left," Tamsyn tells me, as we make our way down the stairs. She locks the door as we exit and we walk hand in hand down the footpath to wait for JP and Scott.

It isn't long before JP's car rolls up to us and we hop in. I give Scott a head nod as we get in and he returns it. We sit in silence all the way to the hospital, lost in our own thoughts. Penny meets us at the hospital entrance.

The familiar sanitary smell hits my nostrils as soon as we enter and make our way to Rafe's room. I don't know if I'll ever get over the association this smell has with Quinn. As we get to Rafe's door, JP pauses before he knocks, pushing the door open. Rafe's parents are sitting to the side of his bed and Rafe is still in the same position as yesterday. He turns to us as we walk in and for the first time we see the Rafe behind the smile first. He looks worn out.

"I'm glad you kids could make it. We know how close you are to Rafe so we wanted to let you know what's happening," Rafe's dad starts. We all stare at Rafe, wondering what's going on.

Rafe takes a big breath in, closes his eyes to steady himself and then opens them and glances at each of us before he softly says, "I'm not okay guys and I haven't been for a while now. The doctors here have managed to secure me a place at Oakley House. It's an emergency suicide prevention programme." I run my thumb back and forth over Tamsyn's hand letting her know I'm here. It hurts to watch our friend in so much pain, but this is a good thing. He's going to get help. "I'm not sure how long I'm going to go for and they want me to go today," he says, and his eyes lock on JP. His best friend. I place a hand on JP's shoulder to let him know I'm here for him too. It's silent for a minute before JP speaks.

"And you'll get the help you need there?" he asks.

"He will, son. It's the best place for him at the moment," Rafe's dad says, as JP and Rafe stare at each other.

"Then that's where you need to be. And we are with you one hundred percent. We only want what's best for you Rafe," Scott chimes in, as he takes a step towards Rafe and grips him in a tight hug.

"Thanks dude," Rafe shakily whispers, as he returns the hug patting him on the back. Scott lets go and Penny steps towards Rafe wiping at her cheeks to clear the tears that have escaped.

"Look after JP for me please?" Rafe says to her, and she nods her head where it's stuck in his neck. When she releases him, his sad face glances at her as she wipes her face. Tamsyn rushes forward and bowls into Rafe's arms, crushing her small body to his and he hugs her just as tightly.

"Shhh, it's okay Petal, I'm okay," Rafe says, as he flattens her hair down on her head and I can hear her sniffles. "Thank you," he softly whispers, which I nearly miss and she lifts her head then leans in and kisses his cheek. He wipes the tears from her face and nods at her in a silent conversation letting her know he's got this. JP still hasn't moved from his spot so I walk around him and hug Rafe myself.

"I'm proud of you man, you got this. And we will all be here rooting for you to get better," I tell him, and he nods against my shoulder. I let go and step back to Tamsyn, taking her hand back in mine. JP still hasn't moved and Rafe's dad picks up on it.

"Hey kids, why don't we give JP and Rafe a minute?" he suggests, as Rafe's parents stand and head towards the door. We turn to follow. Before I exit I turn back and see JP rush to his best friend and all his hurt and anger gets released into sobs. It hurts my heart to see JP so broken but I follow my feet out the door to give them the time and privacy they need together.

About ten minutes pass before JP comes to the door with his red rimmed eyes, telling us Rafe wants to say goodbye so we follow him back in. The somber mood surrounds us as we look at our larger than life friend who looks so defeated.

"I'll be back in no time guys" He says to us, trying to lighten the mood.

"Well we need to get Rafe sorted and then drive him out to Oakley House but we will keep you guys updated through JP so you know how Rafe is getting on," Rafe's dad says. We all nod and then one by one say bye to Rafe. Tamsyn gets another hug off him before we leave and he sadly smiles at us as we go.

The ride back in the car is as quiet as the ride there. Penny left in her car and we drop Scott off home first. As we pull up in front of Tamsyn's house, I'm torn between going with her and staying with JP as I feel like they both need me right now.

Before Tamsyn gets out I say, "Sweetness, why don't you text your mum and let her know you'll be home later and come back to ours for a while?" I hope she can sense that I don't want to leave JP without me having to say the words.

She must catch on as her eyes flick to the back of JP's head before she says, "Sure, that sounds good." She reaches for her phone to text her mum as JP drives away from her house and pulls up at his in no time.

Chapter 7

We hop out of the car and as we enter JP's house, his mum and dad are both there. It doesn't look like either of them went to work today. They look up as we enter.

"Is Rafe okay?" his mum asks.

JP takes a seat on the couch and starts filling his parents in. His mum sits down next to him and pulls him into her arms and JP lets out more tears. I lead Tamsyn to my room to give them some space.

"Will JP be okay? I've never seen him like this before. He looks so lost," she says, as she wraps her arms around my waist.

I embrace her back as I say, "I hope so. We will help him though yeah?"

"Absolutely. How about we watch a movie here? The three of us?" she suggests and I nod.

"Yeah, let's get it set up so it's ready for when JP is finished with his parents," I say, which has Tamsyn jumping on the bed, grabbing the remote and flicking through movies. "I'll go get some snacks while you find something," I say, as I leave her to her search.

As I step back into the hall, JP is getting off the couch so I tell him the plans and he sadly nods following me to the kitchen to make popcorn. He puts some in the microwave to pop while I hunt in the fridge for drinks. I also manage to find a couple bags of lollies in the cupboard which we take with us. Once we get to my room, Tamsyn smiles at us, patting each side of her for us to take our places there. We both sit and I look to the T.V and see she's picked Die Hard. Probably avoided romance because that's Rafe's favourite movie genre. As we get comfortable Tamsyn rests her shoulder on JP's arm while she holds my hand. This beautiful girl is perfect and I meant what I said to her earlier. I'm damn lucky to have her. Hopefully we can help hold JP together until his best friend returns.

Don't Fade. Breathe Easy.

Chapter 8

-- Tamsyn --

It's Wednesday now and all our parents are in agreement about us needing to get back to school so that's what we are doing. They let us have a couple of days off school to process everything but I know Mum wanted me to get back to my normal routine. Walking hand in hand with Tate up the concrete stairs to enter school, he gives it a squeeze to reassure me. The drive to school with JP and Scott was filled with a somber silence. We are all dealing with Rafe's missing presence in our own ways.

Once the bell goes to signal the beginning of the day, I freeze. First Aid is our first class of the day and I don't know if I can face it right now. Tate must sense my apprehension as he gently places a finger under my chin to lift my gaze to his.

A sad smile graces my lips as he says, "It'll be okay. JP and I are with you." I stare back into his eyes for a few minutes before nodding and following him to our First Aid class.

I'm thankful when Lily and Zac start the lesson because we have moved on from CPR. Today we are learning about fractures, strains and sprains. I manage to focus on the lesson and don't let my mind wander to our missing friend. I'm grateful when the class is over and let out a sigh of relief. We only have a few more of these classes and then the life lesson classes will be finished. The class started off exciting and fun but now it makes me nervous more than anything.

We decided not to tell anyone else about what happened with Rafe. His parents were going to inform the school because of all the time he will be missing but we didn't want it getting out to the students. It's the last thing Rafe would want.

We all meet up for lunch and the somber mood seems to have followed us around all morning. We all sit quietly eating our food. My thoughts wander to Rafe and wonder what he's doing and if he truly is okay. It's hard not to notice Rafe is missing. He's usually the one who would be cracking jokes or breaking up the awkward silence but without him here it's like a heavy cloud is hanging over us and none of us know how to deal with it or make it disappear.

The bell for the end of lunch goes and Tate, Scott and I slowly traipse our way to human bio. As Ms. Chadwick starts class, I try to listen by sitting up instead of leaning on my arms. Rafe wouldn't want to be the cause of me not focussing so I try my best. Ms. Chadwick is talking about the nervous system and I catch her glances at Rafe's empty chair with a sad smile of her own plastered on her face. The faculty staff must have already been informed of what happened over the weekend with Rafe. Pain tugs at my heart to think of all the people who would have been affected if I hadn't made it to Rafe in time. I guess he can't see what kind of impact he has on the people around him and that makes my chest tight. I can only hope he gets the help he desperately needs.

While sitting in english at the end of the day, a year nine boy walks in with a note for Mr. Barnes. He hands it to him then leaves while Mr. Barnes reads it. He glances up and lets me know the guidance counsellor Miss Steepleton is wanting to see me. With my brows pulling together,

I pack my bag and shrug my shoulders at Tate, Penny and Scott as they look at me with curious expressions of their own.

"I'll see you in the car park if I'm not back by the end of class," I whisper to Tate as I leave, and trek down the halls to the counsellor's room. I knock on the wooden door with the bronze guidance counsellor sign above it and a few seconds later Miss Steepleton opens it with a beaming smile on her face.

"Welcome Tamsyn. Thanks so much for coming. I didn't drag you away from anything important, did I?" she asks, and I shake my head. She gestures for me to enter and take a seat on the tan couch while she takes a seat on the matching armchair across from me. She folds one leg over the other and then clasps her hands in front of her before she talks. "So Tamsyn, I've been informed about what happened over the weekend with Rafe," she softly says, which makes me wring my hands together. My heart pounds in my chest while I focus on my breathing, willing myself not to get overwhelmed.

"Now I know you may not be ready to talk about it but I want you to know if you'd like to talk then I'm here to listen. I can help you find ways to deal with any feelings that may occur. It was actually your mum who contacted me. She's worried about you and thought it might help if you talked to someone." Inhale, exhale, I keep my breathing steady while she talks. It isn't until I feel the cold on my chin I realise tears have escaped unnoticed. I swipe hastily at them to brush them away.

"I can't imagine what you went through the other night Tamsyn. I do know if you talk about what happened and how you are feeling I can work with you to help you deal with your feelings." She pauses and looks at me with an encouraging smile on her face and the words slip from my lips, needing release.

"I'm just so mad and hurt and upset," I tell her, my anger creeping into my voice. "It's like all these different emotions are swirling around inside me and I don't know how I'm supposed to feel. I'm incredibly sad at the thought that Rafe thought suicide was his only option to feel better but I'm also incredibly angry for the same reason. I just wish he had opened up to someone," I tell her, wiping my cheeks.

"Do you want to tell me what happened that night?" she quietly asks, keeping her full attention on me. I start retelling the story of how I was scared when I realised what he meant and how I ran all the way to the dock in the hopes I was wrong. As I recall what happened after I found him in the water, my words get drowned out by my sobs and she moves to sit next to me, wrapping an arm around my shoulder and handing me a box of tissues.

Once my tears and sobs have softened she says, "Rafe is very lucky to have a friend like you and I'm sure he knows it. I need you to do me a favour though. I need you to ease up on yourself. Let go of the what ifs because Rafe is fine now and he is in the best place he can be at the moment. I don't want you taking this burden on your shoulders. I know it will be hard and the doubts and what ifs will creep into your mind but you need to fight against them taking hold. Do you think you could do that for me?" I stare at her for a minute before I give a small nod.

"Okay, so every time your mind overwhelms you and thoughts like that start to appear, I want you to let them come and focus on your breathing while you release the thoughts away. It's like a mini meditation ritual. It isn't an easy fix, I'm not going to lie to you. But it will help in the long run. And I'd like it if you came and saw me regularly. We can do once a week sessions if you like, and any other time you feel overwhelmed, my door is always open. How does that sound?" she asks hopefully, and I slowly nod again. "At our next session we can check in and see how the meditation ritual is helping." Before I leave I ask her if she could check in with Tate, JP, Scott and Penny too to see if she can help them as well because I know we are all struggling and she says she's more than happy to do that.

Walking to the carpark to meet the others, I feel less burdened than I have since Saturday night and I can breathe more freely. I catch sight of Tate leaning on the side of JP's car waiting for me and a smile drags his lips up when he sees me walking towards him. As I reach him, he wraps me in his arms, delivering a kiss to my lips making me sigh, and I feel less weighed down in his embrace.

Don't Fade. Breathe Easy.

Chapter 9

-- Tate --

On Thursday at school, I am called into the guidance counsellor's office during third period. I haven't been here before so I haven't had the pleasure of meeting Miss Steepleton yet. Her friendly smile welcomes me into the dimly lit room. Her sleek blonde bob frames her heavily makeup filled face as she gestures for me to take a seat.

I know Tamsyn got called into her office on Wednesday and earlier today JP and Scott had their meetings with her. I guess she is going through all of our group. Tamsyn mentioned the guidance counsellor wanted to check in and make sure we were all okay after everything that has happened with Rafe.

"So Tate, I know we haven't crossed paths while you've been at school but I wanted to have a chat and see how things were going. I've been informed about Rafe and I'm just touching base with all his close friends to make sure everyone is okay," she states, all the while smiling at me.

61

I relax into my seat and take a deep breath. My parents wanted me to talk to someone because of Quinn. Unfortunately the therapist my mum booked isn't available for another month as they were fully booked so I could talk to Miss Steepleton until then. She seems pleasant enough.

"What we talk about here, stays in here right?" I ask her, wanting to know my thoughts are safe with her if I say them out loud before I speak.

"Of course Tate. This is a safe space. The only reason I would need to tell someone else is if I thought you were a danger to someone else or to yourself. Anything else is safe with me, okay?" she says, as I stare into her eyes believing her sincerity. So for the first time since Tamsyn, I choose to open myself up to someone else in the hopes I can heal. I'm tired of carrying all this hurt and guilt around all the time. The weight still weighs me down some days and I want to lessen the burden so I can breathe easier.

"Do you know much of why I started at this school?" I ask, staring at her. She changes position in her chair and shakes her head at me in response.

"No, I don't actually know anything about your back story Tate. Would you like to share it with me?" I take a deep breath and nod.

My voice cracks as I say, "I'm a twin. Well I used to be, I guess I should say. I don't even know what I'm supposed to say actually. My twin sister Quinn committed suicide last year but ended up in a coma. She ended up dying a few months ago. So does that still make me a twin or am I just half of a whole now?" I lift my tear filled gaze up to meet hers and I'm met with a heartfelt sigh from her.

"I'm so sorry to hear that Tate. Have you talked to anyone about Quinn?" Hearing her name on a stranger's lips has my heart pounding but I push it out of my thoughts because I need to get used to it. Quinn deserves to be remembered and talked about. I'm doing her an injustice by not mentioning her.

"Not really. Thinking about Quinn gives me panic attacks but they have lessened a bit lately, but sometimes they feel like they might overwhelm me," I say, sadly dropping my gaze.

"Well would you like to come and see me a few times a week Tate and talk about Quinn or whatever else is going on? Panic attacks are nothing to be ashamed about but it sounds like there is a lot going on in your head you probably need to talk through. I promise you, once you voice those thoughts to someone, they won't feel as heavy," she says, her friendly smile directed at me again.

"I think I'd like that. My mum has booked me in with someone but they can't see me for a while as they are fully booked," I tell her, and she nods.

"Well I can see you in the meantime then," she replies. "So it must have been hard for you with Rafe's incident? Did it bring up memories of Quinn?"

I nod as I reply, "All I could think when I heard about Rafe was please, no, not again. I don't think I could handle more pain on top of what I'm already suffering. I've been so worried about Tamsyn I pushed my feelings to the side," I tell her, speaking a truth I didn't even realise I had inside me.

"You and Tamsyn are together?" she asks, and I nod. We haven't put any labels on it but it's obvious to anyone who sees us that we are in fact together. "Well that's totally understandable you are worried about her. I'm sure Tamsyn wouldn't want you bottling up your feelings for the sake of hers though, so try talking to her when things get a bit much. Your feelings are just as valid Tate."

"I just want to protect her, you know?" I tell her truthfully.

"I get that Tate but you also have to look after yourself too. Leaning on each other during the tough times is not a weakness but a strength and it can only make your bond stronger," she tells me. "And Tamsyn is a tough girl, I know she'd want nothing more than to help you too."

"Okay, I'll try talking to her too," I say, which has her nodding.

"So can I ask how you are coping since Quinn and Rafe?" she asks genuinely, wanting to help me.

"I went back home for Quinn's funeral and I wasn't coping at all. It was like I lost all motivation to live. I pushed Tamsyn and my friends here away. I was tired a lot and didn't have the energy to do much," I say.

"Tate, losing your twin must have been incredibly hard. I can't imagine the type of pain it would cause. Would it be alright if I got you to fill in a small multi choice questionnaire? All you have to do is circle one answer. The choices are the same for each question: never, little, some, most or always," she says, and I nod. She walks over to a shelf she has on the far wall, finds the sheet of paper she needs and hands it to me with a pen. I start reading the questions and circling the answers I think relate to me. It takes me a few minutes to finish and then I hand it back to her. It wasn't until the last few questions I figured out what the form was. She calculates my answers and tells me my results.

"So Tate do you know what this form is?"

"A mental health assessment?" I ask, and she nods.

"You landed in the medium range Tate. What that tells me is you are moderately suffering from depression. Did you think you were depressed?" she asks.

"I don't know if I would have thought it was depression. I thought it was just my grief causing it."

"That may be the case, but there can be other factors that contribute as well. Depression can occur for numerous reasons and truth be told, there are a lot of people out there who suffer from depression who don't realise they are. They may feel they have no energy to do the things they normally love, or they start distancing themselves from friends and family. They may also feel empty inside or even sad for some unexplained reason. Depression ranges through a lot of things so sometimes it can be hard to tell if someone is depressed or not. And usually the person has no idea anything is even going on with them so they won't seek help because they don't think they need it," she explains. It sounds so simple and easy coming out of her mouth. I didn't think I was depressed just that I was grieving my sister.

"So if I asked you Tate if you thought you were depressed, what would you say?"

"I would say no," I tell her.

"And do you think Quinn was depressed when she committed suicide?" she asks.

"She had a diary she was always writing in and some of the things she was writing in there make me think she was depressed," I say sadly.

"Do you feel guilty for Quinn, for not seeing that she was depressed?" she asks, and my hands start to shake. It's as if she has pulled the thoughts straight from my head.

"Yes," I whisper, trying to reign in my shaking hands by sitting on them.

"Tate, if you couldn't recognise when you were depressed then how could you have possibly known that Quinn was?" she softly asks, and my defences try to attack my brain.

"Because I'm her twin. I should have seen she wasn't alright. I should have known," I say louder, raising my voice.

"That is a lot of guilt to carry around Tate and I assure you there is no way you could have known. You weren't in her head. Even being her twin, there is no way to know what goes on in someone else's head if they don't express it to you." Her words cause hot tears to burn my eyes. My head and heart hold on to the guilt she is trying to rid me of. "Is this how you feel about Rafe too? That you should have been able to see it in him as well?" I lift my tear filled eyes to her and nod.

"That guilt is misplaced Tate. It isn't your job to know the thoughts of others. You are putting a lot of pressure on yourself." She makes a lot of sense but it's hard to let it go. A lone hot tear escapes and trails a path down my cheek and I quickly wipe it away from my chin.

"Tate, I know that I told you what is said in here stays between us but I'd like you to talk to your parents, if possible. Let them know about the questionnaire and that it shows you have depression. Do you think you can rely on your parents?" she asks.

"Yes, they're great," I tell her, meaning it because I am lucky to have the parents I do.

"Lean on them Tate. I can't speak for them but I'm sure they would want nothing more than to help you. And you do need help Tate. You have been through a lot that most people your age would never go through over the course of their whole life. And I recommend you see a doctor as well to see what they say about the depression too, in case they think you need medication. I could give your parents a ring and talk to them for you if you like?" she offers, and I nod. Pulling out my phone, I give her my mum and dad's cell phone numbers which she writes down.

"So are you happy to come and see me a couple times a week? We can work it around your classes or in your lunch times if you like so you don't miss too much school work?" she offers.

"I'd like that. Maybe one lunchtime and one class period, if that's alright with you?" I suggest, not wanting to spend all my lunchtimes holed up in a therapist's office spilling my guts.

She smiles as she says, "That's fine Tate. I'll work out a schedule and we can organise what works best for you. Now the bell is about to go for lunch so if you want, I can ring your parents at lunch and let them know you've given me permission to call them?"

"Thanks. That would be great," I tell her.

"And thank you Tate for trusting me enough to talk with me." Her warm smile shines at me, putting me at ease. I grab my bag from the floor and fling it over my shoulder as I rise to leave.

"Thanks Miss Steepleton. I'll see you next week," I say, opening the door.

"See you then, Tate."

As I step away from her office, the bell for lunch goes so I head straight to the cafeteria and I'm surprisingly the first in line. I fill my tray and walk out the side doors to our bench in the sun. I exhale and embrace the heat for a minute while I take a seat and wait for the others. One by one, they join me with their own lunch filled trays.

When Tamsyn slides in next to me, I lean down and kiss her neck just below her ear softly whispering, "I missed you," which I do whenever she isn't around. She shivers next to me and rewards me with her perfect smile, making my heart thump loudly in my chest for a good reason this time.

That afternoon my mum gives me a ring, "Hey honey," she says, when I answer.

"Hey Mum, I'm guessing Miss Steepleton gave you a call," I say, jumping straight to it.

"Yeah she did. I knew you weren't coping after Quinn but I thought you were grieving. I didn't think you might be depressed as well," she sadly says, and I catch a sniffle she tries to hide.

"Don't beat yourself up Mum. I didn't think that either. And you did want me to see someone to talk about it so they probably would have picked up on it too," I tell her, not wanting her to feel guilty. There's been a lot of guilt going around and it doesn't help the situation.

"How are you feeling today?" she asks.

"I'm good Mum. It was actually good to talk to Miss Steepleton about things," I tell her.

"She's suggested you see a doctor so I've asked Sharon to organise an appointment for you. She was going to talk to you when she gets home from work," she tells me.

"Okay."

"Honey, I want you to know that you can talk to me and your dad about anything too."

"Thanks Mum. I love you."

"I love you too," she says, before hanging up.

A few hours later after I've finished my homework, there's a knock on my door.

"Come in," I say.

"Hi Tate," my aunty Sharon says, as she pokes her head around the corner.

"Hey," I say, lifting my head from my books, spread out in front of me.

She takes a seat on the bed, looks at me and says, "So I talked to your mum and I've organised an appointment with our regular GP that we see. I've booked you in for tomorrow after school. He's good Tate, we've been going to him for years."

"Thank you," I tell her.

"So I'll finish work early tomorrow and be here after school to take you okay?" she says.

"Thanks," I say again.

She stands to leave but before exiting she turns and says, "And Tate if you ever need to talk, your uncle and I are always here. I hope you know that."

"I do," I say, smiling at her. She nods once then leaves me to finish my work.

The next day at school after Tamsyn and I finish eating our lunch, I tell the others I need to talk to Tamsyn alone. She walks with me away from our table as I lead us towards the school field where we can easily find a spot, far away from other people. We sit opposite each other with our legs crossed.

"Is everything okay?" she asks, her brows pulled together.

"Yeah, I just wanted to talk to you alone," I tell her, before taking a breath. "So Miss Steepleton thinks I might be depressed," I say, letting out my exhale and lifting my eyes to hers. She shuffles closer to me, taking my hands in both of her smaller ones.

"Really? Why does she think that?" she asks.

"I filled out this mental health assessment form and based on my answers, she said I was moderately depressed."

"What does moderately depressed mean?" she asks.

I shrug my shoulders as I answer, "I have no idea. I didn't think there were different degrees to it." I change position and decide to lie on the grass. I pull her back so she lies perpendicular to me with her head resting on my stomach. Both of us stare up into the clear blue sky, lost in our thoughts.

It's silent for a few minutes before she says, "So what's gonna happen now?"

"JP's mum has made an appointment for me with a doctor after school today. I just wanted to talk to you and let you know what was going on."

"You feeling alright?" she asks, her eyes still looking up at the sky.

"Yeah, I thought I was doing better but then I think what happened with Rafe has just set my mind off again," I tell her honestly.

"Yeah I know what you mean. My mind keeps thinking what if I hadn't made it to him in time. I know he's safe now but what if he tries it again and we think he's okay but really he's not," she says, rushing the words so fast I can feel her getting worked up.

"Hey Sweetness," I say calmly, sitting up so her head falls into my lap as she's still lying down. Gazing down at her, I sweep her hair back from her face. "Take a breath. He's okay. At this very moment he's fine," I tell her, as I watch her chest rise and fall as her eyes glisten with unshed tears. She draws a deep breath in, eyes on mine and then exhales. "Let's promise each other we will always let the other know how we are feeling," I say.

"Yeah I can do that. I promise," she says, holding her pinky finger up to me and with my lips tugging up into a smile, I link my pinky with hers.

"Pinky promise," I say, lying back down and closing my eyes. The sun shines on us and in this moment, I let myself relax and try and let my thoughts drift away for a minute.

Later that night when I'm lying in bed, I go over the conversation I had with the doctor after school. He concluded I was indeed suffering from depression. He wanted me to try medication but I wanted to see if the counselling would help first without medication. I have to see him again in a month's time for a progress report and then we will go from there.

I can tell my mum is worried about me from the tone of her voice. She wanted to get on the first flight available and fly out here to see me but I told her there was no need. I reassured her numerous times that I feel fine. I do believe I'm fine or I will be fine, in time. I've got my family and friends I can rely on as well as Miss Steepleton and Tamsyn if I need to talk. So for now, I feel hope. Hope that I'll be okay and get through this and come out the other side even stronger.

Chapter 10

-- Tamsyn --

It's been a couple weeks since Rafe's incident and the weather is getting warmer so Penny invited us around to her place for a swim and then she's hosting a sleepover. I wanted to take my car for a drive even though I can't drive it myself so Tate kindly offered to drive for us. He and JP walked over to my house and then we picked up Scott. It's a tight fit with the guys but they don't mind. Once we pull up to Penny's house, we grab our bags and head inside.

"Hey guys, I'm in the kitchen," she yells from inside her house, so we follow her voice and find her pulling drinks out of the fridge. "I thought we could use the barbeque out the back if you guys want?" she asks.

"Sounds great, Pen. I can get started on that if you like," JP says, smiling at her.

"Cool. I've got some steaks marinating in the fridge and there's some sausages in there too," she tells him. "You guys can just place your bags in the lounge if you like," she says to the rest of us. We walk back into the lounge and place our bags on the floor.

"What can we help with?" I ask, turning back to Penny.

"You can help me carry the drinks and snacks out if you like. Tate and Scott can you guys set up the fold out table that's out there please?" They nod at her and head out to get started. JP follows them to inspect the barbeque before he starts cooking the meat.

"Thanks for having us over Penny. I think we all needed a relaxing day to stop fretting about Rafe. It's been a hard few weeks without him, you know?" I say to her, and she wraps me in a hug.

"He's in the right place, Tam. I'm sure he will be back with us before we know it," she says, and I give her a tighter squeeze. "Let's not dwell on that today okay. Today is for fun," she says, trying to lighten the mood. I give her a small smile as I let her go.

"Table's ready," Scott yells from outside, so Penny and I fill our arms with drinks and carry them out.

"I've got some alcohol in the cabinet if we want mixes?" Penny asks the guys, as she starts lining up drinks on the table.

"Sounds good, Pen," JP says, as he walks back into the house, juggling the steaks and sausages as he returns.

"Tam, do you wanna come with me and we can change into our swimsuits?" Penny asks, so I follow her into the lounge. Grabbing my bag, I walk behind her down the hall to her bedroom. "You can get changed in here Tam if you like and I'll go to the bathroom," she says, as she hunts around in her drawers until she finds what she's after. She pulls out a black one piece and leaves me while she goes to change. I quickly locate my royal blue bikini and change. I'm glad Penny gave me my privacy. I don't know if I'll ever be one of those girls that strips down naked in front of other girls. I finish tying the bikini string around my neck and then shimmy my jean shorts back on. I decide to put my shirt back on over the top but then change my mind. I want to see Tate's face when he sees me so put it back in my bag.

Penny gently knocks on the door.

"Come in," I quietly respond, as she pushes the door open.

Her eyes roam up and down my body making me blush as she says, "Damn girl, you look hot."

"Thanks Pen, you look pretty hot yourself," I tell her, and she does, with her thick black locks hanging down her back. I gather my hair in my hands, running my fingers through it to smooth any bumps before I secure it in a high ponytail. Pinching the ponytail to make it perfect. I leave my bag on her bed as we head back out to the guys. As soon as Penny steps through the door, JP's gaze follows her and I see him visibly gulp before he notices me watching him. Diverting his attention back to the barbeque, I see a slight pink light up his cheeks and can't help a smile igniting on my face. Tate has his back to me, adding more snacks to the table but as he turns his eyes widen as they scan my body. His blatant scanning of my body makes me nervous, but then his lips tug up on one side and I catch a cheekiness shining in his eyes.

Before I can react, he lunges at me throwing me effortlessly over his shoulder in a fireman's hold and jogs to the pool.

"Don't Tate," I squeal, as I can see the plan forming in his head. "I don't want to get wet yet," I tell him, as my little fists pound on his back. He opens the pool gate with one hand while holding my thighs tightly to him with the other. I can hear the other's laughter at the barbeque, finding my predicament funny. Tate stands at the edge of the pool and I try one last effort to get him to release me. "Please Tate," I plead, and he slowly slides my body down his front so I'm standing in front of him. He pinches my chin in his fingers and I see the heat swimming in his eyes. Leaning down, he kisses me until I'm breathless when he pulls away.

"Come on, let's get back to the others," I say, after a few minutes of staring into each other's eyes.

"You go. I'll be there in a minute," he says, and my brows pinch.

Reaching up and touching his bicep I ask, "Everything okay?"

His hand adjusting himself catches my eyes as he says, "I just need to think of my grandma or maybe a hard math problem will do the trick," winking at me, and I cover my mouth with my hand but my giggles still escape.

"Don't take too long," I tell him between laughs, as I lean up and kiss his cheek, leaving him to deal with his problem.

My wide smile is still on my face when I return to the others but they don't mention it as they finish setting up. Tate finally returns a few minutes later, giving me a knowing smile of his own and I can't help the giggle that escapes. It isn't long before JP has finished barbecuing the meat and we dig in. Everyone grabs plates and fills them and we eat in silence which has become our norm of late.

"I heard from Rafe last night," JP says around a mouthful of food, breaking the silence and all of our heads whip to stare at him, waiting for him to continue. "He said he's doing okay and for us not to worry about him. They've put him on some anti depressants and he's going to daily therapy sessions. They want to see how he is going with the medication and stuff first before he comes back home." I let out a sigh of relief because it sounds like he's doing okay.

"That's awesome to hear," Scott says, with a smile spread across his face and I can't help but feel the same.

"He'll be home in no time," JP says, and I wonder if he's trying to reassure himself more than us. He must be missing Rafe like crazy.

"You guys wanna have a swim now?" Penny says, looking around at us, once we've all finished our food.

"Sounds good," JP replies, and we all start clearing away our plates, grabbing our towels and then heading out to the pool. Penny hands around the sunscreen which we all spray on ourselves and rub in. The guys all pull their shirts off and Tate comes up behind me and sprays the sunscreen on my back and gently massages it in for me. I return the favor and then I offer to do Scott's back because JP and Penny are busy doing each other's.

I finish up and then place the sunscreen and my shorts on one of the wooden pool chairs. My eyes glance down to the chair at the end of the row, a small smile lighting up my face as I can't help but think of the night Tate and I talked out here. Seems like so long ago it happened, when in reality it has only been a few months. It's funny how time can play tricks on you, it feels like I've known Tate longer than a few months.

The sound of the water splashing draws my focus as JP's head pops up out of the water and he flicks his hair back and then I spot Scott running and doing a cannonball of his own. I glance at Tate by my side and my finger traces the tattoo on his ribs. His gaze meets mine and behind his smile is a hint of sadness he pushes aside as he grabs my hand and pulls me into the pool with him.

We sink under the cool water, surfacing as I push at his chest as he laughs and grabs my ankle, dunking me again. Penny lets out a scream as she runs and does her own cannonball into the pool and the air fills with laughter as we all enjoy the moment. We all end up splashing and dunking each other, all our worries forgotten for a brief period in time.

"How about we take turns battling each other with one of the girls on our shoulders?" JP suggests, and we all agree. Tate comes to stand in front of me, before he sinks down under the water with his hands reaching up which I take. I lift my legs over his shoulders and then hang on for dear life as he lifts me up. Laughter escaping as I settle above him. We watch JP as he drops under the water behind Penny and then pops his head between her legs and lifts her unaware on his shoulders. The scared look on her face has me and Tate cracking up as she wobbles trying to balance, her hands gripping his head to stay upright.

"You could have given me a heads up," she says, feigning anger as she smacks JP lightly across the head. His bright smile shines at us and he grips her lower legs in his hands.

"Get ready to go down cuz," he says, sporting the biggest grin I've seen on his face in a long time.

"You'll be the one going down," Tate replies, as Scott comes forward to be the referee.

"Okay, on the count of three you can go. And it'll be best of three," Scott informs us, as Penny cracks her neck from side to side like she's getting ready for battle. "One, two, three, go," Scott yells, and the boys move under us and Penny and I grasp at each other with our hands, trying to chuck the other one off. Just when I think I have the upperhand, I go flying backwards off Tate's shoulders as JP managed to out maneuver him. Luckily I manage to close my mouth before I hit the water and come up laughing. I reposition myself on Tate's shoulders and we start all over again. And that's how we spend the rest of the afternoon, everyone taking turns to referee and switching partners. It's the most fun I've had in a long time, but in the back of my mind I can't help but feel Rafe's missing presence.

-- Tate --

After we've spent a few hours in the pool, laughing and carrying on, we get out and sun ourselves on the pool chairs. I reach my hand out to Tamsyn and grasp her hand in mine. I hold her hand as I close my eyes and enjoy the heat from the sun rays beaming down on me and warming me up. I know everyone is struggling with Rafe being gone but this is one of the happiest days we've had in a while and I can't help but smile to myself.

Once we are all a bit warmer, we head inside to have showers and get ready to watch some movies. There are two showers in Penny's place, so while Scott and Penny take one each and JP is distracted cleaning up the barbeque, I thread my fingers through Tamsyn's and pull her down the hallway, away from the others.

When we are out of earshot of them, I push her up against the wall, taking her lips in mine, swallowing her gasp of surprise. Lately my body has been taking control and I need to be as close to Tamsyn as I can. My hand trails down her body, until I cup her butt in my hand, pulling her close to me as she wraps her hands around my neck, pulling her closer still. We get lost in the moment and it isn't until Scott yells, "Shower's free," I regretfully pull away, smiling down at her flushed cheeks. I run a finger down from her temple to her chin, lift her beautiful eyes to mine and my heart overflows with emotion because this girl is mine.

"I love you," I tell her truthfully, and she sucks in a breath as her eyes glisten with tears. She reaches up with her own hand, wiping her thumb over my thoroughly kissed lips and lifts her eyes from my lips to look at me.

"I love you too," she says, and I lean forward, devouring her lips again in another hungry kiss as my heart fills. While kissing her with all the love I feel for her, I thank my lucky stars this girl feels the same way I do. I know we are still young but I don't feel my heart could ever want anyone as much as I want her. Too quickly we are pulling apart again, smiling brightly at each other.

"You go shower, Sweetness. I'll go after," I tell her, and she delivers a chaste kiss to my lips as she walks down to Penny's room, grabs her bag and heads to the shower Scott vacated.

After everyone is showered, we drag a couple of double mattresses into the living room. Tamsyn and I take one and JP and Penny take the other while Scott takes the couch.

"Anyone want a drink? I'm going to make me one," Penny says, as she stands and JP follows her to help.

Before Tamsyn can reply I say, "Hey, I was thinking I could give you a driving lesson tomorrow if you wanted?" as I watch the smile grow on her face.

"Yes, that would be perfect," she squeals, giving me a tight hug. "I'll just drink juice tonight then," she says, as I kiss her lips.

"Can we have two juices please?" I yell, so Penny and JP can hear me in the kitchen.

"I'll take a beer," Scott says, and gets handed one by JP as he sips from his own and hands a glass of juice to Tamsyn. Penny comes over, giving me my glass while she sits back on her mattress with her own drink and we settle in to watch a movie.

Halfway through the second movie, Tamsyn is drifting off but before she does, she turns to me and snuggles into my chest.

Her eyes lift to mine as she mouths, "I love you." My heart leaps with emotion as I mouth it back to her, drawing her tightly into my chest. I feel better than I have in a long time and it's all thanks to my green fairy.

Chapter 11

-- Tate --

The next morning we wake up and laze around on our makeshift beds in the living room, watching a couple more movies before we clean up. It isn't until after lunch we leave and drop off Scott and JP. Once it's just me and Tamsyn in the car, I grab her hand and link our fingers while I drive. I lead the car down towards the dock and as we pass it, we both glance out at it. It always looks so different in the light of day, with the sun bouncing off the water below.

"I miss Rafe," Tamsyn says, as she squeezes my hand tight.

"Me too," I confess. His missing presence is like the elephant in the room when we are all together. His personality is so big, it's hard to not notice he is missing.

"I haven't been able to go to the dock since that night," Tamsyn says. Her confession makes my heart ache as I know she loves the dock. It was a special connection she had to her dad. I'll have to try to help her to rectify the situation.

"We'll fix that, Sweetness," I reassure her, squeezing her hand just as hard.

I pull off to the small side road that runs along the water. It's a twenty zone here and has speed bumps spaced all along the straight strip of road. It's the perfect place for her to learn how to drive. There's a carpark down the far end which she can practice turning too. The water still isn't hot even though the weather is getting warmer, so we are lucky the road is empty for now and not filled with families wanting to go swimming.

"Okay, let's start," I say, as I get out of the driver's seat and walk around the car while she does the same. I tap her butt as I pass her and she gives me a small grin as she catches my eye before we get back into the car. "Do you know anything about driving?" I ask her.

"Not really. I've never driven before so you'll probably have to start with the basics," she tells me, and I nod.

"Okay, first thing's first, seatbelt on and we are going to adjust your seat and mirrors. Move the seat forward so you can comfortably reach the pedals," I tell her, and watch as she adjusts the seat. "Now move the rearview mirror so you can see behind you and adjust the side mirrors with the control on your door." I watch as she carefully does exactly what I said. I take her through the basics, showing her where the controls for the indicator, windscreen wipers and lights are. Once she knows those, I explain about the handbrake.

"Now for your pedals. The smaller one is the accelerator and the larger one is the brake. You use one foot to control both when you need to. You okay with everything so far?" I ask, feeling as if I'm overloading her with information.

"Yeah, I'm good," she tells me, beaming.

"Cool. So we are going to take the handbrake off and start to move okay? Put your hands on the steering wheel," I instruct, and then move her hands slightly higher on each side to what would be ten and two o'clock. "Ready?" I ask, and she nods.

"I'm so nervous, my hands are slippery," she giggles, wiping her hands on her thighs and then repositioning them on the wheel.

"You'll be fine, Sweetness. I'm right here and we'll take it slow to start. Plus no one is around," I say, encouraging her and she nods, more sure of herself.

"Okay, so press down on the brake and I'll release the handbrake for you to start." She looks at me after she puts her foot down so I click the handbrake and lower it down to release it. "Now put the driveshaft into drive then move your foot down to the accelerator and gently press on it. It might take you a while to get the feel for the brake and accelerator," I tell her. She gently pushes down the accelerator and we slowly move forward.

"Keep your hands steady so we stay in a straight line," I tell her, so we don't start swerving all over the road. I glance at the concentration on her face as the car moves at a snail's pace and try not to laugh. "Push a little harder on the accelerator Sweetness, you can do it," I encourage her, trying to get her to relax.

As she presses down we zoom faster and her squeal has me saying, "Ease up, not so fast." I hold back my laugh at the expression on her face when she realises she's pushed too hard. Suddenly I rock forward as she presses down hard on the brake, giving me an uneasy look.

"Sorry," she shyly says, biting her lower lip.

"It's okay, Sweetness. You are learning and you are doing pretty good for your first time behind the wheel. So keep going. Slowly press down on the accelerator again and ease into it," I tell her, and this time her pace is a bit smoother and we manage to travel all the way to the end of the road with no hiccups. I instruct her to turn into a parking spot but she ends up parking between two spots. We will have to work on parking next time. I pull the handbrake back up and I'm mesmerised by the excitement I see, blazing in her eyes.

"That was so much fun," she squeals, as she throws her arms around my neck, pulling me closer to her for a hug.

"You did good baby," I tell her, as I breathe in her scent which grounds me. I release her as I say, "Lets go again," earning me a smile from her. We spend the next hour with her going up and down the straight road. I have to reverse it for her a few times to get it into position as she's struggling with turning but apart from that, she does great for her first time. We finish the lesson with some important information about blind spots. I get out of the car and walk around it to demonstrate blind spots. I get her to track my movements and take note of where I disappear from sight so she understands how important checking all her mirrors are.

Once the novelty of her first driving lesson wears off, we change seats and I drive us back down the small straight road and turn onto the main strip. As we close the distance to the dock, I pull over to park which has her looking at me, with her brows furrowed.

"Why are we stopping?" she asks. I move my gaze out her window to stare at the dock that is still being hit by the late afternoon sun.

She follows my gaze and is silent for a minute as her stare lingers out the window before she quietly says, "Okay."

"I'll be with you the whole time," I tell her, as I unbuckle my seat belt and exit the car walking around to her side. I take her hand and we cross the road together. Her hand is getting slippery cupped in mine so I release it and drape my arm over her shoulders, pulling her into my side as she wraps an arm around my waist. We walk silently to the old wooden dock. I'm hoping in the light of day it won't be as bad for her. Her steps slow the further along we go and I match her speed.

Two metres away from the edge and her feet stop as if they are glued in place. I glance down at her. Her wide eyes stare out at the blue water below the dock and I can hear her forced breaths as she tries to keep them even. I shuffle behind her, pressing my body flush against her back, folding both my arms over her collarbones and drawing her head against my chest.

Chapter 11

I kiss the top of her silky hair and whisper, "I'm here, Sweetness," as I let her work through her thoughts in her own time, hoping I'm giving her strength.

The silence draws on as we stand there, staring out at the water. The setting sun still shines brightly down on us as it lowers in the sky. I don't know how long we stand like that but I don't hurry her and eventually she breaks the silence.

"Do you think he knew what was going to happen when he came out here?" she quietly asks.

"I don't know. Only Rafe would know that Sweetness but that doesn't matter because he's okay now," I tell her, squeezing her closer to me.

"Do you think I'll ever stop seeing him face down in the water?" she says, sending a shiver through her body.

"I hope so Sweetness. Can you try to think of memories of your dad instead?" I ask, trying to get her mind off Rafe.

"I'll try," she replies. I don't want her to lose this place and not come out here anymore because even though she doesn't remember, to me this is our place. It's the place where I met her all those nights ago. Even though she doesn't have the same memory I do, I don't want her to give up the dock.

The sun lowers more and a chill in the air surrounds us.

"You ready to head home?" I ask.

"Yeah, thanks for bringing me Tate. Maybe if I keep coming out here it won't be as bad," she sadly says. She turns around in my arms and presses her ear to my chest, where my heart is like she's listening to it beat.

"I hope so," I softly say, gripping her chin to bring her gaze to mine as I lower my lips to hers. As she opens her lips to mine, I force all the love and strength I have to offer into the kiss, hoping she feels it. I crush her to me before we pull away a few minutes later, completely out of breath. The first smile she's had since we stepped foot on the dock graces her lips. I can't help but return it as I grab her hand and lead her back to the car.

We pull up at her house and I park the car in the driveway since I'm going to walk home. Before I leave, I deliver another kiss to her plump lips then head down the footpath in the direction of JP's house. My heart beat runs rampant in my chest. I'm thankful I have this beautiful girl in my life who is helping me heal, without even realising what she does to me.

Chapter 12

Chapter 12

-- Tamsyn --

The school holidays come around fast and Rafe still isn't back. He's sent the odd text or two but I haven't talked to him since he left. I know he rings JP once a week as JP updates us on how he is doing but it's not the same. The good thing to come out of this all is Rafe is doing better. I just wish I could see for myself to know he was okay.

It's the Saturday after school let out and Tate and I are in my kitchen, eating some egg salad sandwiches I whipped up for lunch. My mum walks in while we are eating and asks if we have plans for the holidays and I shake my head because my mouth is full of food.

"Umm, I was actually wanting to talk to you about that," Tate says, gazing between my mum and I. I raise my brows in question because I have no idea what he's about to say. He shifts on his seat before he speaks, putting his half eaten sandwich down on his plate. "So my parents rang me this morning and they wanted to know if I could come back home for a week or so of the holidays. They organised for Quinn's headstone to get made and it was finished earlier than expected. They wanted to have her unveiling while I'm on holiday so I don't miss any more school," he says, and my heart deflates a bit at hearing he'll be gone for part of the holidays.

I push my feelings aside because now is not the time for a pity party when he should be focussing on his sister's unveiling.

I give him a bright smile as I say, "When do you leave?" trying to project to him and my mum I'm fine.

He turns to my mum and says, "Well I was actually wondering if Tamsyn could come with me?" and my heart stops. I would love nothing more than to go with Tate but it also makes me nervous about going to his hometown. I set my eyes on my mum to see her expression and she gazes back at me.

"Would you like to go?" she asks me, and I nod enthusiastically, which draws a smile to her face.

"I talked to my parents and they offered to pay for Tamsyn's flight too," Tate tells my mum, but she shakes her head.

"No that's fine Tate. I can pay for Tamsyn's ticket. Can I get your parents' number so I can give them a ring to discuss this?" she asks, and Tate gives her their number which she dials from the landline then and there.

I glance at Tate and he gives me a wink as we listen to my mum introduce herself over the phone.

It isn't long before she's laughing and then she peeks at me and Tate before she says, "Yes, they are a bit inseparable now, aren't they?" and I know she's talking about us. "No you don't have to do that," she says, and then, "Fine, okay that sounds like a plan. I'll let them know. Thank you, Jessica. It was nice talking to you," she says, before she hangs up on Tate's mum.

Looking at Tate, she says, "Your mum is going to book the flights for tomorrow if she can. She's looking at them now." I leap out of my chair and straight into Tate's arms. "Your mum also wouldn't let me pay for Tamsyn's ticket but I'll give you some spending money instead bub for you to take with you."

"I can really go?" I squeak, not believing it.

"Yes you can go. As long as you two behave. And Tate I'm trusting you to look after her," she tells him, sternly but with a hint of a smile. "Your mum will ring you soon with the flight details and I've asked her to email them to me as well. I'll drop you two off at the airport. So off you go, you better get packing in case you leave tomorrow," she tells me, as she ushers me out of the kitchen. I jump out of Tate's arms and give my mum a tight hug with a whispered thanks in her ear. Turning to Tate, I offer my hand which he takes as I drag him up the stairs to help me pack. I pull my old purple suitcase out of the hallway cupboard and Tate carries it back to the room setting it on the floor by my bed.

"What do I need to pack?" I ask him, flustered.

He steps towards me, staring into my eyes saying, "I don't care. I'm just excited I get to spend the holidays with you after all," before he gives me a deep kiss. I have to disengage myself from him after a minute or else we will never get me packed. With my heart feeling lighter than it has in a long time, I move to my dresser and start pulling out clothes to go in the suitcase. Tate shows me how to roll them up to help save space plus stop them from wrinkling so much.

I walk into the bathroom and pull out a toiletry bag I fill with a few things like deodorant, my hairbrush and face moisturiser. Tate tells me not to worry about anything else as they have it at his house. I leave the toiletries on top of my suitcase to put my toothbrush in before we leave.

I can't hide my excitement as I leap into his arms and wrap my legs around his waist when he catches me.

"I'm so excited to see where you grew up," I tell him.

"And I can't wait to show you around. Pierce and Xander will be so happy to finally meet the girl I keep texting them about," he tells me, with a big smile on his face, his green eyes twinkling at me.

"Well, I think I'm done. Do you want me to come help you pack?" I ask him, and he shakes his head.

"No, I already packed this morning after my mum rang me. I was just hoping you would be allowed to come too," he tells me. So we decide to snuggle down on the bed and watch a movie instead while we text Penny and Scott to let them know we won't be around for the week.

-- Tate --

My mum rings me on Saturday night to let me know she managed to get us on a last minute flight for Sunday. Tanya drops us off at the airport and I hold Tamsyn's hand through the whole flight. It's nice to have her all to myself for a bit. I'm both nervous and excited to show Tamsyn around where I grew up. As we walk through the airport, I catch sight of my parents waiting off to the side for us. Mum starts crying as soon as she sees me and my only thought is to stop her tears. I let go of Tamsyn and jog the last few steps to Mum and pull her tightly into my arms, while she squeezes me back.

As I let her feet hit the ground, she wipes the tears from her cheeks as I give my dad a quick hug too.

I step back beside Tamsyn as I say, "Mum, Dad this is Tamsyn. Tamsyn, these are my parents."

"Hi honey, it's so good to finally meet you," Mum says, pulling her into an embrace which Tamsyn nervously returns then she waves awkwardly at my dad.

"Yes, nice to meet you, Tamsyn," Dad says, taking her suitcase for her so I hold her hand, hoping I'm comforting her.

"It's nice to meet you too and thank you so much for having me to stay," she gushes.

"It's no problem. We are happy you could make it," Mum says, smiling at her.

In the car and on our way home Mum says, "So we have booked the unveiling for Friday. Your father and I have taken the day off work. You can ask Pierce and Xander if they'd like to come if you want. It isn't going to be too big."

"Yeah, I'll ask them Mum. I haven't actually told them I was coming back. I wanted to surprise them," I say.

Tamsyn leans into me and whispers, "You and your surprises," which has me smiling at her.

As we drive through the familiar neighbourhood, the big red door comes into view and my heart starts pounding. I wonder if I'll ever be able to look at the front door without it making me want to run away. I breathe out and steady myself as we get out of the car, grab our suitcases and turn to walk up the path.

"I love this door, it's so beautiful," Tamsyn gushes, as she stares at the reminder of Quinn. My parents turn to glance at me before they walk through with sad smiles on their faces.

"Quinn actually picked out the colour," I tell Tamsyn, her head whipping my way, taking in my expression.

"Well she had good taste," she says, reaching out and squeezing my hand. I lead her through the house to my room and push open the door. My brows squeeze together as I take in the mattress on my floor, all done up like a spare bed. I put our suitcases on the bed and then tell Tamsyn to wait in my room while I go talk to my parents.

"What's up with the mattress in my room?" I ask them, as they are in the kitchen making coffee.

Mum turns to me and says, "I don't think Tanya would appreciate her teenage daughter being under our roof and sharing a bed with you for a week?"

"But I always sleep in Tamsyn's bed at her place and Tanya doesn't mind," I tell them, and I realise it may not have been the smartest comment to let slip out of my mouth.

"Well that is there and this is here. Tanya has trusted us with Tamsyn for the week so please just give me this for peace of mind," she says, as she closes her eyes squeezing the bridge of her nose. I glance at my dad who has busied himself with the coffee and catch a glimpse of him hiding a laugh. I don't say anything, just wait for Mum to open her eyes. When she does she says, "It's either the mattress on the floor or you sleep on the couch. We don't have a spare room and I'm not ready to disturb Quinn's room yet," she softens, and the fight leaves me.

"Okay Mum, the mattress is fine," I say. Her glassy eyes shimmer at me as she nods.

"Do you kids want a coffee or hot chocolate?" Dad asks, trying to change the subject.

"I'll take a coffee thanks. I'll go see if Tamsyn wants one," I say, turning and walking back to my room to find Tamsyn sitting on my bed, taking in my room.

"Sweetness, would you like a coffee or anything?" I ask her, and she nods, following me back to the kitchen. I direct her to sit at the table while I fix our coffees, remembering how she likes it.

We all sit down for the rest of the afternoon while my parents ask Tamsyn questions to get to know her. They met her briefly when I returned to JP's but they don't know much about her except she's the reason I desperately wanted to return to live at JP's place.

After we both take showers, we settle on the couch to watch some movies while my parents disappear to their room to give us space.

Chapter 12

Tamsyn curls her feet underneath her and leans into my side as I drape my arm over her shoulders, pulling her close. We decide to surprise my friends tomorrow with my appearance.

It isn't until halfway through the second movie Tamsyn's gentle snores alert me to the fact she's drifted off. My mum comes in not long after and sees her sleeping next to me.

"She seems like a great girl, I can see why you couldn't stay away," my mum says, squeezing my shoulder. "Why don't you take her to bed and remember to sleep on the mattress and leave the door open."

I slide my arm under her legs and lift her effortlessly into my arms, carrying her down the hall to my room. Her soft sighs into my chest has my heart beating faster. Man, I love this girl I think as I gently place her on the bed and pull the covers over her. She looks so peaceful with her chocolate waves fanning out over my pillow. The urge to climb under the covers and pull her into my chest is strong but I don't want to upset Mum so instead I drag the mattress right next to the side Tamsyn is on, getting as close to her as I can. Listening to her soft sleep noises, I drift off easily for the first time in a long time.

"Aren't they just the cutest, James?" I hear my mum whisper, while I force my sleepy eyes to remain shut. My arm is at an awkward angle and I can feel Tamsyn's hand in mine.

"Oh, to be young and in love for the first time again," my dad says, wistfully.

"Hey, we aren't that old," she scolds my dad, playfully.

He chuckles as he replies, "Remember when we were that age and I would sneak in your window?" which causes my mum to giggle. I haven't heard them this playful in a long time. It's nice to hear but I hope they move on before they say something gross that haunts me forever.

"Shhh, don't be giving your son ideas. Let's leave them to sleep," Mum says, and their voices drift away the further from the room they get. I peel my eyes open and follow my hand. It grasps Tamsyn's hand as her arm dangles from the side of the bed and she's as close to the edge as she can get, without falling off. I manage to sit up without disturbing her, still clutching her hand. I move the hair from her face to get a better view of her. My lips draw me closer before I can stop myself, kissing her smooth skin softly. It causes her eyes to flutter before they open, a smile gracing her face.

"Morning," she whispers.

"Morning Sweetness," I reply, before I drag her down onto the mattress with me. I pull her into my chest which causes us both to sigh and then crack up laughing. I don't think I'll ever get enough of this girl. "I love you," I tell her, as her eyes look into mine.

"I love you too," she replies, giving me a kiss but before we can deepen it, Mum walks by fake coughing and breaks the moment. I lean my head backwards, staring up at her upside down while Tamsyn tries to move but I hold her in place.

"Morning Mum," I say, giving her my biggest smile.

"Come on you two. Come and join us for breakfast since you're awake. I've made pancakes and coffee," she says, as she walks away.

We get up and I pull Tamsyn into a quick hug and whisper, "I think my parents are worried about us spending too much time in bed together." I look into Tamsyn's eyes and give her a wink which has her blushing. I didn't think my parents would be this hardcore at trying to prevent me and Tamsyn from having sex. I'd never taken them for cockblockers. Not like I'd want my first time to be with my parents around anyway so they have nothing to worry about.

"So what are the plans for today?" Dad asks, while sipping his coffee.

"I think we are going to surprise Pierce and Xander and spend the day with them if they are free," I tell them, around a mouthful of pancakes and syrup.

Chapter 12

"You'll like them Tamsyn, they're good boys," Mum says.

We finish up breakfast, brush our teeth and get changed and form a plan. I'm not sure how to surprise the guys but Tamsyn has an idea.

We walk hand in hand over to Pierce's place after I texted Pierce to see what he and Xan were up to. I don't think he suspected anything. He said they were just playing video games at his house so it's perfect.

Once we arrive at Pierce's, I hide behind the hedge on the side of his property while Tamsyn waltzes up to the house and knocks on the door. I peek through the foliage and can see Pierce when he answers the door.

"Hey, can I help you?" Pierce says, as leans on the door frame, crossing his arms over his chest looking Tamsyn up and down with a furrowed brow.

"Hi, my car broke down and I was just wondering if anyone could help me?" she says sweetly, rocking on her feet.

"Xan," Pierce yells over his shoulder, and a few seconds later I see Xan's face appear in the door.

"Well hello there, good looking," he says, flirting with her. I can't wait to see his face fall when he sees she's mine.

"She said her car broke down and needs some help," Pierce tells him, and Xan's eyes light up.

"Well, you've come to the right place. I'm your man. How about you show us your car?" Xander says. He's been tinkering under the hood of cars since he was a toddler because his dad is a mechanic. It was the perfect way to lure them out of the house. As they follow Tamsyn away from the house over to the hedge, I see Xander checking her out from behind and elbowing Pierce.

As they get closer to the hedge I creep down and once Tamsyn passes, I step out into their path yelling, "Boo" making them both jump back.

"Tate!!" they both scream at me, as they gather me into a hug together.

"What are you doing here?" Pierce asks, as we all disengage.

"We came back for Quinn's unveiling." I tell them, the air growing somber.

"We?" Xander asks, and I pull Tamsyn out from behind where she's been hiding.

"Guys, this is Tamsyn. Tamsyn, this is Pierce and Xander," I introduce them.

"The green fairy?" Xander says in awe, and Pierce pulls her into a hug followed by Xan.

"I knew you looked familiar when you came to the door. I just couldn't figure out where I'd seen you before," Pierce says, remembering the picture on his phone from when Avery had tricked JP into sending one.

"What's a green fairy?" Tamsyn asks quietly, looking at me.

Xander links arms with her and says, "Well let me fill you in," and I smack him over the head.

"I'll fill you in later, Sweetness," I tell her, pulling her into my side away from Xan and kissing her head. The guys stare at us, with stupid grins on their faces.

"You hanging with us today then since you're here?" Xander asks.

"Yeah, that's the plan," I reply.

"Let's go do something then. Show Tamsyn around," Pierce suggests, and I nod.

"Sounds good," I say, and we head back to Pierce's house for them to turn the game off and lock up. Our local shopping mall isn't too far away so we walk over. On the way, the guys fill Tamsyn in on stupid stories of us growing up, which has her clutching her stomach from laughing so hard. It makes me wish these two were always around me.

We spend a good hour walking around the mall. We grab some slushies and sip on them as we walk and talk so Tamsyn can take in the shops.

"Ooh let's go ice skating," Xander suggests, as we get to the end of the long mall strip where a big ice skating rink is set up.

"Yay, I haven't been in ages," Tamsyn squeals, and I can't help but let her excitement seep into me.

I pay for all our passes and we grab our different sized skates and change into them. We are all a bit shaky to start as none of us have skated in a while but once we skate around a bit, we are more confident. There aren't many other people on the rink so it gives us the perfect opportunity to race each other. Our laughter fills the air as we speed around chasing one another. I race Tamsyn and as I get closer to her, I grab her hand and we slow down. I pin her to the side of the rink, leaning down and kissing her because it's been too long without my lips on her. We get so lost in the moment, it isn't until my brain registers Pierce and Xan cheering and hollering I break away from Tamsyn and they start laughing. I glance at Tamsyn as a blush creeps up her cheeks, and we start racing again.

Walking home, I can't remember the last time Tamsyn and I laughed so much. It makes me more determined to keep her beautiful smile permanently etched on her face. She deserves to smile after all she's been through. A fleeting feeling of guilt surfaces at being this happy while Quinn isn't here but I push it away, not wanting it to wreck the day. Saying goodbye to the guys, we make plans to hang out again tomorrow.

When we get back to my house, my parents tell us they have plans to catch up with Dad's business partner and his wife for dinner. It was planned weeks ago so they can't get out of it. Mum gives me money to order some pizza and tells us they won't be too late home.

As they're walking out the door, she sternly says, "Keep your door open," with a glint of a smile on her face and I roll my eyes at her as I shut the door. We order pizza and sit down on the couch to watch a movie.

Halfway through the movie Tamsyn says, "So are you going to tell me what this green fairy business is?" and I turn to her with a blush flushing my face. I squeeze the back of my neck as I prepare to tell her.

"Well the guys always give me a hard time about being a virgin and one time, they were joking about me waiting for a princess in a far away land. I let it slip that it was actually a green fairy I was waiting for," I say, causing her brows to pull together.

"I don't understand," she says.

"You don't remember the first night we met but you were wearing a green dress. When you turned around to face me, I couldn't help but think you looked like this magical green fairy," I tell her gulping. "So they know it's you I've been waiting for," I say, honestly.

"Oh," she says, biting her lower lip between her teeth.

"No pressure or anything. I wasn't going to say anything but since the guys mentioned it and you wanted to know. It doesn't change anything but I do want my first time to be with you whenever that is, whenever we are ready," I tell her, embarrassed. It's hard to talk about sex stuff with her.

"I'd like that too," she shyly says, and my heart nearly bursts out of my chest.

"When we're both ready," I tell her, not wanting to pressure her and I want it to be perfect. She nods and leans in for a kiss and I open my lips needing to taste her. Our confessions have electrified the air and we are both needy for each other. I lie down on the couch, pulling her on top of me. She runs her hands under my shirt, so I yank it over my head, one handed. I clutch my shirt in my hand and stand up carrying her as her legs wrap around my waist. We continue kissing as I make my way to my bedroom and lower her to my bed.

I lean over her and stare into her eyes and my heart overflows with emotion. I didn't think I'd feel this way about a girl but she does it without even trying. She peels her t-shirt off and lays under me in her pink lace bra.

"Not sex but I want to be close to you," she softly says, pushing the hair off my forehead. I nod as I take her mouth in mine and our hands roam each other's bodies. My thumb grazes over her nipple in her bra and her hips jerk up towards me. It makes my dick strain in my jeans harder than it already was. I sit back on my knees and flick the button on my jeans open and unzip them while Tamsyn does the same to hers. I step out of mine and lay back down in my black boxers and shimmy Tamsyn's jeans off her legs, throwing them on top of mine. I stare down at her in her pink underwear in awe. This perfect girl is mine which has me letting out a contented smile.

"You're perfect," I whisper, as I hold her eye contact.

"I love you," she says, as she links her legs around my hips, pulling me towards her.

"I love you too," I say, my lips meeting hers and my dick grinds into her. I've never gone this far with a girl before. I have never let myself get carried away. With Tamsyn, I could get lost in her forever. Our moans fill the air as I rock back and forth against her. I pull her nipple free from her bra and take it in my mouth.

"Tate," she murmurs. She sounds like she's worshipping my name so I continue licking it.

"Is that good baby?" I ask, unsure.

"So good," she says, so I carry on more confidently. I grind harder and faster against her as I lick her nipple and run my thumb over the other one.

"I'm close," she says, as I suck harder and grind faster, following my own release.

"Tate," she says, as her body starts to shake and I look up to watch her face. Her closed eyes with her mouth forming an O, makes me come right along with her. I drop my head into her neck, kissing her there as my release fills my boxers.

My weight presses down on her, as the euphoric feeling takes over and I smile into her neck then lazily lift myself up to take in her expression.

"Hi," she shyly says, with a giddy smile on her lips.

"So, that just happened," I say, and we both crack up laughing. I roll off her and pull her into my arms, trailing patterns on her bare back with my fingertips.

"Did you come too?" she softly asks, and I look down at my now wet boxers and smile, not even embarrassed.

"Yeah I did. I'll have to clean myself up," I say, her eyes follow my gaze to my soiled boxers and she starts giggling. "You think that's funny, do you?" I taunt her, which has her squealing under my arms as I pin her to the bed with my weight, making her squirm.

We are both out of breath from laughing as I take her lips quickly in mine again whispering, "I love you,".

"I love you too, so much," she replies. I kiss her nose as I jump up and tell her I'm going to shower. The smile lighting up my face can't be wiped off the whole time I wash myself clean. When I get back to the room, I see Tamsyn has slipped some pajamas on and is tucked into bed fast asleep. I drop a kiss on her forehead and quickly pick up our discarded clothes and put them in the washing basket so my parents don't know anything went on. I sink down onto the mattress on the floor and with a big smile on my face and a contented heart, I drift to sleep.

Chapter 13
~

-- Tamsyn --

The last few days with Tate have been amazing. It's the happiest we have both been the whole time I've known him. I still can't believe what we did the other night. Unfortunately now that we have opened pandora's box, it is only making me want him more. We've spent a lot of time with Pierce and Xander but I don't mind as they are great and I can see how close Tate is with them. I am dying for some more alone time though.

It's Wednesday and his mum showed me a whole bunch of photo albums of when Tate was little. Tate was so embarrassed, especially of the photos with the questionable haircuts. I went along with it though as I could see how much it meant to his mum. She was lost in the nostalgia of it all. Most of the photos contained Quinn in them and more than once, her eyes got glassy retelling stories of the two of them. Quinn was the splitting image of Tate. She was beautiful and even though I didn't know her personally, it's hard to think about what happened when she was surrounded by so much love. I guess that's the thing about depression. It can affect anyone, rich or poor, loved or lonely, and it's nobody's fault.

The more days I spend in this house, the more I notice they don't have any recent photos up. Most of the ones they have around are of Tate and Quinn when they were younger so a plan quietly forms in my head.

My plan solidifies when I hear Tate's mum say, "That's one of the last photos we have of the four of us together," while I'm looking at a candid shot someone has taken. Tate's dad is kissing his mum on the cheek while Tate and Quinn have their heads thrown back laughing. They look so happy. It makes my heart hurt for the fact they will never be together like that again. They will never be whole again.

Tate's mum asked him to help her prepare lunch so while they are busy, I quickly take the photo out of the album and carefully put it in my bag. We have lunch and then I ask Tate if we can go to the mall.

"I want to do something for your parents for letting me stay," I tell Tate, as we walk to the mall.

"You don't need to do anything Sweetness, they are happy to have you here."

"I know but I want to do something nice for them. And I want to keep it a surprise so you can't see either," I tell him.

"Is that so?" he says, smirking.

"Yes it is. So how about you go grab us some slushies while I get this sorted and I'll meet you there?"

"Okay Sweetness," he says, kissing my temple before he heads one way and I quickly go in the opposite direction.

I walk into the camera and photo store and go straight to the counter asking if they can help me with what I want. I pull out the photo and hand it over. They tell me it will be ready for me to pick up tomorrow. I pay and thank them as I leave in search of Tate. As I get closer to the pop up slushy store in the centre of the mall, I notice Tate standing to the side with a slushy in each hand. What makes my feet stop is the fact there are two girls there, talking to him. It isn't until I catch a glimpse of one of them, I recognise her. She's the same girl from the photo. With my heart pounding, I stare at Tate and can see the anger on his face while the girl talks. His frigid posture lets me know he wants nothing to do with these girls.

My only thought is of getting Tate away from them. Before I can stop myself, I walk up to them with a huge smile on my face. Tate sees me coming and his body relaxes. Not caring about the girls being present, I press my lips to his.

"Sorry I took so long," I say, staring into his eyes. He hands me my slushy and I take a big sip as he slips his arm over my shoulders, pulling me close.

"That's okay, Sweetness. You ready to go?" he says, blatantly ignoring the girls.

"Yeah."

"Aren't you going to introduce us?" the girl from the photo asks, smirking at me.

Before Tate can say anything I say, "I don't really care who you are, not after the way you treated Tate. Maybe you should run along and fix your chipped manicure before someone notices. And on another note, leave my boyfriend alone."

She glances at her fingernails quickly and I can't help but smirk at her as her face reddens and a scary vein pops out by her temple. She looks like a volcano ready to explode as Tate and I walk away laughing.

"That wasn't too harsh, was it?" I ask Tate, when we are out of earshot.

"That was perfect. I take it you recognised Avery from the photo?" he says, guilt leaking into his voice.

"Yeah, I did. You looked angry when I saw you so I thought I'd save you," I tell him, laughing.

"That was epic. I've never seen anyone put Avery in her place before," he says, the smile stuck on his face.

"Well they don't call me the Ice Queen for nothing," I tell him, and we both throw our heads back laughing.

"Well I've never seen this Ice Queen you guys talk of, only my little ball of Sweetness," he confesses, which has my heart gushing as I snuggle closer to his side. "Did you finish what you needed to?" he asks.

"Yeah, I can pick it up tomorrow," I say, and he nods. We walk back to his place laughing and finishing our drinks.

On Thursday morning, we walk over to the mall and again I ask Tate to go in the opposite direction so he doesn't see the surprise. When I get to the store the lady shows me my order and a smile ignites on my face. I hope they like it and I haven't overstepped. She wraps it in some black tissue paper for me so Tate won't see then she places it carefully in a bag.

Tate tries to peek into the bag on the way home but I don't let him. Once we enter the big red door, we get a surprise of our own when JP jumps out of Tate's bedroom at us.

"Hey guys," he says, picking me up and swinging me around as I laugh.

"You never said you were coming?" Tate says, as he fist bumps him.

"Dad managed to get work off for a few days so we flew over this morning. We didn't want to miss Quinn's unveiling."

"That's awesome. I'm glad you're here," Tate says, and we head into the kitchen where Tate and JP's parents are all sitting at the table, drinking coffee and catching up. With both their mums sitting next to each other, you can see the similarities between them.

"There you two are. I was wondering when you'd be back," Tate's mum says.

I wasn't planning to do this now but since everyone is around I take the opportunity. I walk over to Tate's parents and nervously place the bag in his mum's hands.

"I just wanted to say thank you for having me to stay. I hope this is okay," I tell them.

"You didn't have to get us anything honey. We are glad we've gotten to spend time with you," his mum says, as Tate comes to stand next to me.

"Open it Mum, I'm dying to know what it is," Tate says, giving my hand a squeeze. His mum pulls out the present and peels back the tissue paper. Her breath hitches as the huge photo canvas comes into view. The small photo of the four of them blown up looks beautiful. Everyone is quiet for a beat and then his parent's eyes meet mine and I can see the unshed tears, waiting for release. They both stand quickly and pull me into a hug as Tate squeezes my hand harder.

"I hope it's okay," I say, as they release me, both wiping their cheeks.

"It's perfect Tamsyn. I've been meaning to put more photos up of Quinn but I haven't gotten around to it. This is very sweet of you. I know the perfect place to hang it too," she tells me, as she shows JP and his parents.

Tate pulls me into his own hug, his face hidden in my neck as he whispers, "I really love you, you know that?" He delivers a kiss to my bare skin before he pulls away, looking deep into my eyes.

We spend the rest of the day talking and listening to stories before JP's parents leave to go to their hotel. JP stays to hangout with Tate and I, watching movies and eating junk food. He ends up crashing on the couch for the night. Before we go to sleep, Tate sits on my bed and pulls me into his lap so I'm straddling his thighs.

"You really are something else," he softly says, before kissing me.

I pull away before we get too carried away. JP's snores coming from down the hallway help to break the moment. We separate and move into our own beds, the pounding of my heart lulling me to sleep.

-- Tate --

Friday rolls around faster than I would like. My parents have organised for the unveiling for later this morning so we've got time before we need to get ready. It's only going to be a small occasion with my family, JP's family, Tamsyn, Pierce and Xander.

After breakfast, Tamsyn and I shower and get ready. While she's brushing her hair I come up behind her, wrap my arms around her waist, lean my chin on her shoulder and stare into the mirror.

"You okay?" she asks, looking at me in the reflection of the mirror.

"Yeah. I just know it's going to be a hard day," I tell her, feeling my emotions already spiralling all over the place. She places her hairbrush on the dresser and folds her arms over mine. "Do you want to help me with something, Sweetness?"

"Sure. What is it?"

"Well do you remember me telling you about Quinn and me making daisy chains? I wondered if you'd help me make some for her today?"

"Of course. I loved making them too when I was little." I kiss her temple before turning her in my arms and grabbing her hand, leading her outside to the backyard.

We are in luck. The green grass is scattered with daisies. We sit cross legged with our knees touching and get to work. We work quickly but carefully to put the little slit in the stem and slide another stem through the hole and repeat.

"How's this?" Tamsyn asks. I look up and my breath catches. My mind flashes to an image of Quinn. A daisy crown sits upon her blonde hair cascading over her shoulders, the biggest smile lighting her face. I shake my head and the image disappears. My heart thunders in my rib cage and when I look up, I am staring at the gorgeous brown haired girl in front of me. Keeping my breaths steady and not letting the panic control me, I feel my lips pull up in a sad smile.

"It's perfect, Sweetness. Quinn would have loved you," I tell her, letting the weight of the day settle over me. Tamsyn scoots over and climbs into my lap, pulling my lips to hers.

"What was she like?" she gently asks, as we carry on with our delicate work.

I gather my thoughts and while focussing on threading daisy after daisy through the tiny holes, I talk about my sister, my twin.

"She loved colour and all things bright. She was kind and sweet and would do anything to help someone in need. She was also a bit of a daredevil too, always up for an extreme challenge. She loved big and had the biggest heart of anyone I knew." I take a breath to compose myself as I continue. "My favourite thing about her was this smile she would make. When she was trying to contain her laughter, her whole face would light up, her face would turn red and you'd catch a glimpse of the happy tears trying to escape her eyes. I'd give anything to see one of those smiles again," I sadly say, leaning my chin on Tamsyn's shoulder as we focus on the flowers. Our piles of daisy crowns, growing.

"I know it probably doesn't help and it's not the same but if you can hold that image in your head, you'll be able to see that smile whenever you need her," she softly says, and a lone tear runs down my face.

"Thanks, baby," I say, meaning it. Tamsyn and I connected over our grief and experiences but we are so much more than that. I never would have gotten through this without her shining light helping me out of the darkness. I hate to think what would have happened if I had taken the darker path.

We keep working silently, lost in our thoughts and not thinking about how many daisy crowns we've made. I glance at the growing pile and an idea forms. I place a crown on my head while Tamsyn still wears hers and then I count to make sure I have enough for everyone.

Once we head inside to join the others, I hand them out. Mum and Dad get teary eyed when they place them on their heads, knowing how much she loved these simple flowers. I even have one each for Pierce and Xander and hand them out to them when they arrive for us all to leave.

When I catch sight of her headstone, my feet remain planted, taking it all in. It's a black marble with white writing etched into the stone. It says 'Quinn Ivy Devereaux. Sunrise 9th May 2001 to Sunset 25th March 2019. Beloved Daughter, Sister and Friend. Loved beyond measure.' A white angel is carved into the side, it's huge wings spread wide and curling in to embrace it while the angel's head is bowed. It isn't all that, that holds my attention though. It's the shimmering stained glass rainbow that sits at the top of the headstone I can't take my eyes off. I'd forgotten Tamsyn was next to me until I feel the squeeze of my hand.

My eyes meet my parents and I sadly say, "It's perfect. She would have loved that rainbow."

"We had to include some colour for her," Mum says, as Dad wraps an arm around her, pulling her closer. We all stand quietly in our own thoughts. Pierce, Xander and JP all put different flowers into the flower holders at the front of the headstone and it brightens it up even more. The windmills we put down for her birthday are still there, they've just been moved into their own holders on the side too.

My Mum pulls me around to the back of her headstone and I read the words, 'Just whisper my name in your heart and I will be there,' and it opens the floodgates. I burst into tears in my mother's arms as she does

Chapter 13

the same. Releasing all the emotions we have inside into our embrace. One by one the others come around to see the inscription on the back and I see them all wipe away stray tears of their own.

Before we leave, we all remove our daisy crowns and place them gently onto the corners of the headstone or amongst the flowers so she's surrounded by the simple pleasure she once loved so dearly. As we all leave to head back to the house for a dinner and night of remembering Quinn, I lean down and press a kiss to my fingertips and transfer it to the angel, holding my hand there.

"I love you, Quinny," I say into the breeze, and with one final glance back at her grave I release a breath then take Tamsyn's hand and let the silent tears fall, unashamedly down my face.

Don't Fade. Breathe Easy.

Chapter 14

-- Tamsyn --

On Monday we flew back home and my mum picked Tate and I up from the airport. JP and his parents flew back yesterday. I could tell Tate was a bit sad about leaving Pierce and Xander. You can clearly see the bond the three of them share. They came to see us off at the airport and gave me big bear hugs before we left. I'm going to miss them a lot, for the simple fact they made Tate laugh the most I've ever seen.

My mum has taken a few days off work to spend some time with me. So on Tuesday she takes us to get haircuts she booked for us. I only get a trim as I like having my long hair. Mum goes a bit drastic and gets her shoulder length hair cut into a short bob and gets some highlights put in. It's a huge difference but looks great on her.

As we are walking around window shopping, I build up the courage to ask Mum something important that's been on my mind. We've always had a close relationship so I know she would want me to talk to her about this.

"So umm, Mum, I was wondering if you could take me to get on birth control?" I say, rambling. I can't see her initial reaction as her back is turned to me as she looks into a clothing store.

She whips around startled, staring at my face as I bite on my lower lip, "Have you." she starts.

"No, not yet. I'm still a virgin. I just want to be prepared," I tell her, and she visibly relaxes.

"Well, I'm glad you came to me first bub. Of course I can do that. How about I see if we can get you an appointment today while we are out?"

"That sounds great, Mum," I say, relaxing myself.

"So I'm guessing you are thinking about you and Tate having sex?" she says casually, and there goes my relaxed composure. Back to awkward.

"Mmhmm," I mumble, and she throws her arm around my shoulder.

"It's a big step bub. I can see how much Tate cares about you and I'm glad you've come to talk to me first about it. Do you want to know what my mum said to me when I was in your position?"

"What?" I ask.

"She said if you aren't able to talk about sex in a serious way without feeling embarrassed or awkward then maybe it's not the right time to be having sex. She said this because with sex, you are trusting someone completely. And you need to be able to have conversations with them about safe sex and boundaries and stuff," she tells me.

So I put on my big girl panties to prove I'm ready and say, "Okay, I want to have sex with Tate," and both our cheeks redden.

"Just remember that you can stop at any time as well. First times aren't usually known as being the best. But it's good that you are wanting to be prepared. I'll ring the doctor now and see if there's any appointments free today," she says, as she pulls her phone out of her pocket and starts dialling. After chatting for a minute she says, "They can squeeze you in for an appointment in half an hour, so how about we head over now?"

"Sure," I tell her, as we make our way to the car and drive to the doctors.

My doctor is reassuring and extremely nice about the whole thing. We decided to try me on the pill and see how it goes. She said sometimes it takes a while before women find the right method of birth control to suit them so I have to keep track of any side effects. I can start taking it but it won't be effective until I've been taking it for a week. It's not like I'm going to jump Tate as soon as I see him. She also gave me a brown paper bag filled with different condoms causing me to blush. This is feeling more real now I have taken this first step.

We grab my pills from the pharmacy on the way home and when I walk into my room, I stow the pills and condoms in my bedside table. Once the drawer is open I catch sight of all Tate's notes and pull them out, scattering them on my bed. It all began with these notes. My heart always feels so full when I think of Tate and I hope that feeling never goes away.

Later that night, I'm nestled in my bed watching movies on Netflix. I told Tate I needed to spend time with Mum since I was away the first week of the holidays. I haven't seen him since we got back but he's been texting me non-stop.

When the movie is nearly finished a text comes through so I open it smiling.

Tate: Hey Sweetness, what are you doing?

Sweetness: Watching a movie, what about you?

Tate: Standing outside your front door like a creeper. I miss you.

My heart thunders in my chest and I quickly reply.

Sweetness: I'll be down in a min

I quietly throw the covers off and slip into my black leggings, a hoodie and sneakers. I glance at the clock and it's just after ten o'clock so Mum could still be awake. I stealthily tiptoe down the stairs and out the front door where Tate greets me with a bright smile.

"Damn, I've missed your face," he says, hooking his hands under my thighs and lifting me into his arms, squeezing me tight as he nuzzles my neck. He walks away from my house carrying me.

Once we are far enough away from home I say, "You can put me down now. I have legs you know," trying not to laugh at him.

"Why walk when I like carrying you? You feel good in my arms," he says, with the biggest grin, delivering a kiss to my lips which makes my heart flutter. "Look here we are," he says, letting me drop to my feet, my gaze following his. I stare down at the grey concrete that has now hardened. I haven't been back to see it. To be honest, I had completely forgotten about it. Staring back at us is the 'TNT' he carved into the wet concrete. It seems like a lifetime ago since that particular night.

"Still looks perfect," I tell him, as he takes my hand but something causes his brows to pinch together.

"It would be perfect if it had forever on the end," he whispers, as if he didn't mean to say it out loud. He gently tucks a stray hair behind my ear as my heart gallops out of my chest.

"Is that so?" I say, just as quietly, staring into his eyes.

"It is. I've tried to live without you before and I'm a hundred percent sure I don't ever want to do that again," he admits. He swallows my reply with his lips, devouring my mouth as we wrap our arms around each other. As we break away, he takes my hand tugging me towards

112

the playground and we both take a swing, letting our weightless bodies soar in the dark.

"What have you been doing the last few days?" I ask him, as I pump my legs to swing higher.

"Not much. Missing you mainly. JP and I have been playing on the Xbox and eating our weight in junk food," which has us both laughing. "What have you and your mum been up to?" he asks, knowing I was spending time with her and I blush in the dark hoping he can't see. I slow my swing and plant my feet and turn the chains, holding the swing to face him.

"Well we went to the doctors today," I say, and it has him stopping his swing too.

"Is everything okay?" he asks, worry leaking into his voice.

"Yeah it is. I just asked if I could go on birth control," I tell him, my cheeks burning under his gaze. He holds my gaze as we sit in our swings, facing each other. "I wanted to be prepared," I tell him, and his mouth pops open.

"I love you," he blurts, and I giggle.

"I love you too," I say, as I get off my swing and stand between his open thighs. He reaches his hands out, holding the back of my legs.

"We don't need to rush," he says, staring into my eyes.

"I know, but I wanted to be prepared just in case. She gave me a big bag of condoms too," I tell him, trying to not be awkward, taking my mum's advice. If I can't talk about it with Tate then how can I take the step of giving myself to him fully.

"I want it to be perfect," he says, gulping. This is the most we have ever talked about it.

"How come you haven't had sex already?" I ask, curious.

"I've always wanted it to be with someone I cared about. I don't know where the idea came from but it's stuck with me. I've never cared about someone like I do about you," he softly says, rubbing his palms against the back of my legs, pulling me in closer. "What about you?"

"I'm not sure. I was with Blake for so long but every time he wanted to, it didn't feel right. It felt like something was missing. I'm glad I never had sex with him now," I tell him.

"Me too," he says, a lopsided smile shining at me.

"I'm nervous it will hurt," I confess.

"I don't want to hurt you so we will take our time and can stop at any time okay?"

"Okay," I say, feeling safe with Tate. He pulls me onto his lap and starts swinging. The chains creak under our weight. "Tate, it'll break," I squeal, trying not to laugh as we soar higher. I loop my arms around his neck holding on.

"It'll be fine," he says, smiling at me as his legs pump harder. We swing higher and I hold on tighter, fearing we will fall but believing Tate would never willingly put me in danger. Tate's gaze stays on my face the whole time. "I'll always keep you safe," he says, and I lean forward, igniting a kiss.

We continue to swing with our love surrounding us, lost in the moment. As Tate walks me back home, he gives me a kiss before I sneak inside. I go to sleep with a smile plastered on my face I don't think will ever be erased.

-- Tate --

On Wednesday morning I bite the bullet. JP's parents are both at work so it's just us guys. I sit next to JP on the couch while he is consumed by shooting people on the Xbox.

"Hey bro, can I ask you something?" I query, wiping my sweating hands along my shorts to wipe the moisture off.

"What's up?" he asks, his eyes never leaving the screen.

"Umm, how badly does sex hurt for girls the first time?" I blurt out.

"Whaaat?" JP screeches, as his focus leaves the screen and his character gets shot. I lift my burning face up to look at him and his wide eyed expression. "Oh man, you're asking me for sex advice?" he asks, looking squeamish himself.

"Yeah, well I don't wanna ask Dad or your dad," I say, scrunching my face up while he does the same as he thinks about talking to his dad about sex.

"Well, I don't know. I've never been with a virgin. I have heard it hurts though."

"Anything else you can tell me?" I timidly ask.

"Man, you know who you need... Rafe. He's good at this stuff. And I know he's been with a virgin before because girls beg him to have sex with them," he says, laughing sadly. I can tell he misses his best friend although he doesn't say it much. "You could text him, but he doesn't always reply. I think they are only allowed their phones once a week or something."

"Nah, that's okay man. Can I ask about your first time?"

He laughs loudly as he leans back, intertwining his fingers behind his head.

"Honestly, my first time was a mess. I didn't know what I was doing and I'm pretty sure my hands were shaking because I was so nervous," which we both laugh at. "Are you and Tamsyn thinking about it?" he asks, after the laughter dies down.

"Yeah," is all I say.

"How about I text Rafe and ask him?" JP asks.

"Can you pretend it's for you though?" I say, not wanting more people to know about Tamsyn and I.

"Sure," he says, as he pulls out his phone and starts texting. "Okay, I said hey bro, hope you are well. Can you tell me how to deflower a virgin without hurting her," his eyes flicking to me with a blank face as I punch his arm.

He cracks up laughing before reading me the real text, "I'm kidding, I'm kidding. I said I'm going to have sex with a virgin. Need help stat. Happy?"

"You're a dick sometimes," I say, laughing myself. "You think he'll reply today?"

"Not sure. It seems to be random when he gets given his phone. You wanna play on the game with me while we wait?" he asks.

I nod, grabbing the spare controller and sink back into the couch, settling into a game. It's half an hour later when JP's phone starts ringing.

"It's a private number," he says, so I focus on the game knowing it's not Rafe.

"Hello," he says, answering. "Bro, whose phone are you ringing from?" he asks, with a huge smile taking over his face as he mouths Rafe to me. I forget the game and focus on JP. "You good bro?" he asks, as he nods along to whatever Rafe is saying. "Good, good," he says, then he's quiet for a bit and his eyes glance at me before he cracks up. "How did you know?" Then he laughs some more before handing me the phone.

"Rafe?" I say, into the phone.

"Hey dude, man so good to hear your voice. How you been?" Rafe asks me.

"Good man. We are all good here. You doing better?"

"Yeah man. I'm on medication now that is working so I'm feeling a lot better. And seeing a therapist is helping. How's Tamsyn doing?" he softly asks.

"She's good man. Worried and missing you but she's good."

"That's good to hear. I miss her too. I owe her my life," he sadly says. He lets out a sigh before he says, "So that's why I don't want you botching up her first time," which makes me choke on air.

"What?" I play dumb.

"I know JP wasn't asking about him. You two are idiots. He's so into Penny he can't see straight and she said herself she isn't a virgin." I slap my head because we both hadn't thought about that before we sent the text to Rafe. "Okay so straight to the point. You and Tamsyn are thinking about having sex?"

"Yeah," I say, as I feel my face heat.

"Well main things you need to know. Take it slow and make sure she is in one hundred percent. Foreplay is your friend. And lastly dude I've seen how you and Tamsyn feel about each other, have fun and you'll be fine," he tells me, sincerely.

"Thanks man," I say, smiling into the phone.

"I better go dude, but tell everyone I said hi."

"Bye, man," I say, hanging up.

"You good now?" JP asks, staring at me.

"Think so. Sorry Rafe had to go before I could give you the phone back."

"All good bro. He said he had to charm one of the supervisors to use the phone quickly since he's out of credit until the weekend." His reply has us both laughing because it is definitely something Rafe would do. "And he knew as soon as he read the text it wasn't about me," he says, which keeps our laughter going. We all miss Rafe being around. I just hope he returns soon and fills the void he created.

Chapter 15

-- Tamsyn --

We finished off the holidays by having a sleepover at mine on Friday night and then spent Saturday lying around watching movies. No one was in the mood to do much else, knowing we were back at school Monday.

As we enter school on Monday morning, there are a few teachers at the gate directing all the seniors to the hall for an announcement. The guys and I direct ourselves that way and bump into Penny who joins us. Tate and I walk hand in hand and I notice that Penny walks next to JP. He's whispering things in her ear for only her to hear which has her cheeks turning pink.

We all take seats in the hall and wait for the rest of the students to join us before our principal Mr. Astle takes centre stage, behind the microphone.

"Welcome back to term three students. We are now half way through the year so I want to make sure everyone is working hard at their classes and completing the necessary assignments to make sure you get the best marks possible. This term we will be setting up individual sessions with the careers advisor to make sure you are on the right path. They will help you look at options for next year in regards to University and Tafe. Now is not the time to be slacking off but instead to be putting your head down and studying harder," he states, while he glances around seriously at all the students trying to get his point across.

"In saying that, this term we are going to be hosting our senior camp trip." Whoops and hollering fills the hall as the excitement levels rise. I'd forgotten about the senior camp they have every year.

"Quieten down," he says, raising and lowering his hands, gesturing us to be quiet but you can still feel the buzz of excitement in the silence. "As I was saying, the camp will be this term. We will be handing out the forms as you leave today. There is a permission form and a cost for the camp so make sure you give it to your parents as soon as possible so you don't miss out. There is also a list of items you may need that we've suggested. This year's camp will be a few hours away at a resort in the countryside and past years have had a lot of fun in these camps so I hope you can all make it." Whispers fill the hall as the excitement is hard to contain.

"The life lesson classes have finished so we will be reverting back to your time tables from term one as well. I won't keep you any longer. Please head to period one and grab a form on your way out." Everyone shuffles out of their seats, grabbing their bags and we are passed a yellow form on our exit. I glance over the sheet and see the camp goes from Monday to Friday. There's also a two hundred dollar fee to pay for everything per student. I fold it up and tuck it into the front pocket of my bag as Tate grabs my hand and we walk to English.

Mr. Barnes starts off the class by giving us an assignment. I guess Mr. Astle was right. Now is not the time to be slacking. We are getting more work than ever piled on to us. He explains that every lesson we are to take five minutes to write down something we are grateful for and near the end of the year we are to do a presentation based on what we have written down. Our presentation will be scored on our speech, creativity and effort put in and will go towards ten percent of our final grade for the year. He has us start straight away so we have to flip to the backs of our books and write something we are grateful for. Tate's hand squeezing my thigh while his eyes stay glued to his book has me smiling down at my own work. The only thing I can think to write is Tate.

At lunch time the intoxication from everyone's excitement over camp lingers around our table.

"Camp is going to be so good. I can't wait," JP says, as he bites into his sandwich.

"What activities do they usually do?" Tate asks, sitting across from me, digging into his own lunch.

"They usually have things like abseiling, high ropes courses, and kayaking. I know one year, they even got to go look at glow worms in some caves," Scott tells us. Chatter ensues around the table with everyone wondering what we will get to do. I take a bite of my own sandwich and have to stop myself from choking when I feel a foot sliding along my bare calf. I peek up at Tate who is suspiciously very invested in his plate of food with a cheeky smile on his face.

Well two can play this game. I kick my shoe off and run my sock covered foot up Tate's leg and then right between his legs which has him coughing over his tray and Scott having to pat him on the back.

"You alright man?" Scott asks him.

"Yeah, just went down the wrong pipe," he says to Scott, while he finishes coughing, his pink cheeks turning my way while I smugly smile at him. He wipes the smug smile off my face when he grabs my foot under the table, and holds it against his hardening length while we stare into each other's eyes. Our silence goes unnoticed by the others as they are too busy talking about camp. Tate's eyes flutter closed and I watch his chest as it rises and falls while he tries to keep himself composed.

I wiggle my toes and his eyes fly open, dripping in lust as he tilts his head to the side indicating we should go. I drop my foot from his lap and wiggle it back into my shoe while Tate grabs his bag, his nearly full tray of food forgotten.

"Hey guys, we forgot something we had to do. We'll catch you later," he says to the table, as he grabs my hand and I quickly grab my own bag as he drags me away from the table, laughing.

"Whatever you say, bro," we hear JP yell, as the chuckles from the table reach our ears knowing exactly why Tate is dragging me away from them. His fast pace has me jogging to keep up with his long strides as he leads me into the toilets around the back of the hall, which hardly get used. As he pushes inside, he checks the stalls are empty then locks the main door and pushes me up against it, taking my mouth with his.

"Damn, you drive me crazy," he whispers, as his lips descend down my throat as his body weight presses me further into the door. His hand snakes under my skirt grabbing my butt and squeezing, which has me moaning into his mouth. With our tongues tangling, I can feel his hardness pushing into my stomach.

"You started it," I defend with a smile, as his mouth comes back to mine. Our hands slide wildly over each other, needing to touch as much of the other as possible. His lips suck hard on my lower neck and I know he's leaving a mark. Then all too soon he releases me, taking a step back as we calm ourselves. Resting his forehead on mine, our breaths tangle as we breathe the other in. After a couple of minutes he steps back and uses his palms to flatten my hair back as it's out of place.

"You might need to fix it," he says guiltily, so I step in front of the mirror and take in my reflection. My cheeks are flushed and my hair is all loose and sticking out from my ponytail so I pull the elastic band out and retie it. Tate comes up behind me, wrapping his arms around my waist, and leaning his chin on my shoulder. "Have I told you how beautiful you are today?" he says to my reflection, which makes me smile.

"You're trouble," I tell him playfully, which has him scoffing.

122

"I think you are the one who is trouble," he says, as he turns me in his arms and pins me against the sink. "I can't think straight when you're around," he says, as he leans in to press a soft kiss to my lips.

"I think you're thinking with the wrong head," I say blankly, trying to hold in my laughter but he tickles my side and it lets loose. The ringing of the bell saves me from his torment.

His eyes drift to my neck and I see his pupils widen, "You might need to cover that?" he says, spinning me back around to face the mirror. Pulling my shirt to the side I see the red hickey he's left behind.

With a smile on my face I button my top button up to hide it, "All hidden," I say, smiling at his reflection.

"Let's get out of here before we get carried away again," he says, kissing the back of my head. Leaning down we pick up our bags we dropped in our flurry. He unlocks the door and pulls me out, kissing my temple before we head off in different directions. We both turn around at the same time which makes us both smile before we turn around and walk away.

-- Tate --

A note gets delivered to my math class after lunch and it's Miss Steepleton wanting to see me. I grab my bag and make my way there. Knocking on the door, I enter and take a seat. We spend the session talking about how my holidays were and going through the emotions I felt about Quinn's unveiling. Some days are harder to cope with than others but I feel by talking to Tamsyn and Miss Steepleton, the weight doesn't press down on me as much. They've lightened the load and I know it's okay to feel the way I do. I'm still coming to terms with what Quinn did. I don't know if I will ever accept it but for now I'm thankful the thought of her doesn't send me into a panic any more.

After school I give my mum a ring about camp and fill her in on the details. She's going to make the transfer for the fees directly to school and tells me I need to get JP's parents to sign the permission form.

With that done, I settle down on my bed to start on my homework but get sidetracked by Quinn's diary, poking out from under my pillow. It's been a while since I've opened it up and after the conversation with Miss Steepleton today, I want to feel closer to Quinn. I flick through the pages and lose myself in her words before I finally close it again. I can only handle it in small doses. I don't want to let it overwhelm me or bring up painful memories when I have so much work to do. Pushing it back under my pillow, I focus on my homework for the rest of the evening.

Chapter 16
~

-- Tamsyn --

This week has been one of those weeks. It's on fast forward, the week whizzes by and before you know it, it's almost over. It's been filled with an electrifying current in the air as everyone is buzzing with enthusiasm for our camp. I can't wait. I haven't been to a camp since before I started at high school. It was a three day camp and wasn't very action or adventure filled.

I've started taking a proper interest in my classes and paying attention to what the teacher is going over during class. I've let the year slip away while drifting in and out of my fog of grief but I want to knuckle down and focus now. I don't want to be repeating my last year of school if I can help it. I think Tate is in a similar situation with switching schools as it's thrown him off a bit as well so we've decided to try study sessions together. I'm thinking we may need to enlist the help of Scott too to get us on track. He may need to act as a chaperone too so we don't get distracted.

Sitting in human bio for the end of the week I say, "Should we have a sleepover tonight?" to Tate and Scott.

"Sounds good to me," Scott says, keeping his eyes on the board while he takes his notes down.

I feel Tate's hand squeeze my thigh as he says, "You know I'm always down for a sleepover," which sends tingles over my skin. I smile down at my book as I'm sure he can feel the heat coming off my face. He always knows what to say or do to make me blush.

I gather my lust filled thoughts of Tate and push them to the side and say, "I was thinking maybe you could help me study or point me in the right direction for my assignments please, Scott?" turning his way.

His eyes light up at the unexpected question, "Sure, I'd love to T. If you need help too Tate, I'm more than happy to help you both get back on track."

"Thanks man, that would be great actually," Tate says.

"We could have a big study session before our usual movie marathons?" Scott suggests.

"Sounds like a plan, Stan," I say cheerily, which has Scott nudging me with his shoulder. A big smile across his face.

The bell signalling the end of the day goes and everyone rushes to pack their bags and race out of class for the weekend. As I'm packing my own bag, Tate takes my hand and sharp paper edges poke into my palm. I open my hand to find a small white folded piece of paper. I glance at him as he looks down at me with an easy smile gracing his face. I peel it open and there in red ink is a big heart with the word 'my' above it and 'belongs to you' under it. I know my face is back to being a ruby red before my eyes even meet his.

"And mine belongs to you," I say, leaning up on tippy toes to deliver a chaste kiss on his lips. Back on my flat feet, we stare into each other's eyes before Scott banging on the desk has us both jumping apart.

"I swear you guys could stare at each other all day without blinking," Scott's amused voice says. We finish collecting our things and I carefully place Tate's note in my skirt pocket before we walk out to meet JP by his car.

He's with Penny, leaning against his car so when we are closer I say, "Are you guys up for a sleepover? We are gonna do a big study session before any movies though," filling them in on the plan.

"I'm in," Penny says, glancing at JP to hear his answer. He gets distracted by his phone which he pulls out of his pocket. Opening up what I'm guessing is a text, his eyes widen with a hint of a smile on his lips.

Shaking off whatever the text said, he says, "Sure I'm in too," before he leans in and whispers something in Penny's ear before she nods at him. Tate and Scott take no notice of JP and Penny as they pile into the car and I follow, telling Penny I'll see her soon.

JP is distracted the whole journey home and we pass Scott's street without him turning into it like we usually do. "Umm, JP you missed my street," Scott says, glancing at JP from the passenger seat.

"Oh, umm, that's okay I need to go home first," he mumbles, like his mind is somewhere else. I glance at Tate and he shrugs his shoulders, none the wiser about why JP is acting so strange. We pull up to JP's house and he turns the car off and opens his door. "Out you guys get," he tells us, which has us all looking at each other, clueless about what's going on. It's even more suspicious when Penny pulls her car up to park behind him and we wait for her to get out.

"Don't look at me, he just told me to follow you guys," she says, shrugging her own shoulders. JP quickly leads us into his house and as soon as he opens his door, his face turns side on and I see the biggest smile I've ever seen cross his face as he dashes into his living room. We follow and then all stare in shock for a minute taking in JP wrapping his best friend in a big bear hug. Rafe.

"Rafe," I squeal, as my legs race to him, leaping into his arms as he pulls away from JP to catch me, swinging me around.

"Hey, Petal," he laughs, kissing me on the cheek before he places me on my feet again. He then hugs Scott, Tate and Penny while we all stare at him.

"You're back?" I timidly ask, my heart unsure if it sees Rafe or he's a figment of my imagination. It's been so long since we last saw him.

"Yeah, I'm back. I've finished my time at Oakley House," he tells us, as his and JP's parents walk down the hallway to us. His parent's beaming smiles look so different to the defeated looks they had the last time I saw them in the hospital.

"We were gonna head over to Tamsyn's for a sleepover and some studying. Are you able to come?" JP asks, his eyes flicking between Rafe and Rafe's parents.

Rafe looks to his parents for permission then his dad says, "That's fine son. How about we take you home first and drop you over shortly?"

"Sweet. I'll meet you guys there," Rafe says, and we all nod.

"Tate, you wanna get ready then we can go?" JP says.

"Yep, I'll just jump in the shower," he leans over, and kisses me on the head before he walks towards the bathroom.

"I'll head home first then meet you guys at Tamsyn's too," Penny says, as she waves goodbye and leaves. Rafe and his parents leave and I can't help but feel a twinge of sadness at watching him exit the house. It's been so long since we've seen him and it's like my heart doesn't understand we will be seeing him shortly.

Before I realise what I'm doing, I'm running out the front door.

"Rafe?" I call, as he's reaching the car with his parents. He turns at the sound of my voice and his smile drops once he sees my face. We both rush to each other and he wraps his arms around me.

"I'm okay Petal. I'm really okay this time," he whispers into my hair, knowing what I followed him out here for. I cling to him, worried if I let go he will disappear. A few minutes pass as we hold each other, needing this moment.

As we break apart I ask, "You're sure you're okay now?"

He tilts my chin up with his fist so he's staring into my eyes, "I promise. And I won't ever lie to you about it again. Deal?" he says.

"Deal," I reply.

"Now get your butt back inside so I can head home and meet you guys at your house," he says, with a slight smile on his face. I nod once as I turn my back on him and walk back inside.

Scott is already seated on the couch so I join him to wait for Tate and JP. My eyes nearly bulge out of my head when Tate walks past moments later with a black towel wrapped around his waist. Droplets of water drip from his wet hair. More droplets run down his bare chest as he turns to us. I catch sight of the tattoo on his ribs which always makes me want to trace my fingers over it. When my eyes finally finish ogling him he smirks at me, winking before he opens his door and disappears behind it. When he reappears, he's using his towel to dry his hair one handed while dressed in a red t-shirt and black basketball shorts.

It isn't long before JP joins us, his bright smile still plastered on his face from having his best friend home. We drive over to Scott's and wait for him to get ready and then drive over to mine.

"Don't tell my mum yet guys. I want her to get surprised," I tell them, before we enter the front door.

"Hey Mum," I yell out, and she comes out from the kitchen. Ever since Dad died she cut her hours down at work so she works school hours. No more late nights at the office for her.

"Hey bub, are you guys having a sleepover?" she asks, knowing it's our usual plan of action for a Friday night.

"Yeah we are going to do some studying this time too," I tell her proudly, and it has her smile widening.

"That's awesome to hear," she says, looking at each of us.

"Penny will be here soon. Can you let her in when she arrives please?" I ask Mum, as we all walk up the stairs to my room.

"Of course. I'm just finishing off some baking so you guys can have a snack shortly," she says, heading back towards the kitchen.

We enter my room and start pulling out our books and spreading them out. I slip my hand into my pocket, pulling out Tate's note before I place it gently into my bedside table with the rest of the collection.

"Bub, Penny is here," Mum calls, and we race to the banister to see her reaction. It hasn't been long enough for Penny to get ready so it must be Rafe. We quietly watch as Mum opens the door. Her hands shoot to her mouth to cover her shock as Rafe enters and wraps his arms around my mum. She squeezes him back and I can see the tears in her eyes as she looks up at him when he releases her.

"I'm so glad you're okay," she says to him, as she cups his face with both hands.

"Me too, Tanya," he says, his own tears swimming in his eyes. He hugs her again.

Mum must feel us watching as her eyes flick to us leaning over the banister and she says, "You knew?" accusing us and we crack up laughing.

"Yeah, we just saw him at JP's," I say, as Rafe picks his bag up off the floor he had dropped and starts trekking up the stairs.

"Well I'll make some extra chocolate brownies or something," she says, smiling as she disappears to the kitchen again, knowing brownies are Rafe's favourite.

Penny arrives half an hour later and Rafe fills us in on his time at Oakley House. We all settle into our school work, all working on different subjects but Scott helps where he can. We decide to try and keep this study group going twice a week at least so we can all catch up on work. Rafe's teachers were sending his work to his parents so he was able to get all his work done while at Oakley House so at least he isn't behind. One less thing to worry about.

Mum calls us down to try her baking after we'd been studying a while. She's gone all out for Rafe's surprise homecoming. She has made brownies, cupcakes, shortbread and even a massive quiche for us to share. After we gorge on everything delicious, we head back upstairs and decide to set up the mattresses before we continue with the studying. Scott is in charge and cracking the whip while keeping us on task. I have put his birthday present to use and now all his notes he'd photocopied for me are all neatly arranged and color coordinated. It makes it a lot easier to keep track of everything now.

After working so hard on our school work, we reward ourselves with a movie.

"Rafe, you can pick tonight," I call to him, from my spot on the bed with Tate.

Rafe scans through the movies until he comes across one he likes. He clicks on 'Love and Basketball'. So we all snuggle down to get comfortable and enjoy the movie.

"Do you think he's okay?" I whisper to Tate, while my chin rests on his bare chest and he gazes down at me. One hand tucked under his head while the other is aimlessly rubbing up and down my back.

"I hope so. It's hard to tell with him, you know?" he whispers back.

"Yeah I know." He leans forward and plants a kiss against my forehead and then pulls back to look at me.

"We'll keep an eye on him. Don't worry, Sweetness," he says, so I turn my attention back to the movie and try to focus on what's happening on the screen.

It feels like five minutes later and I'm being shaken awake.

"Petal, wake up," which has me waking up gasping for air, trying to calm myself after my latest nightmare.

"Rafe?" I ask, not believing he's in front of me for a second.

"Yeah it's me. You okay?" he asks.

"Yeah, just a dream," I tell him. I peek over to Tate who is still fast asleep, his gentle snores filling the air.

"Wanna come downstairs and talk for a bit?" Rafe asks, so I nod and follow him down the stairs to the living room couch. The exact same spot I once talked to Tate after his nightmare.

When we are seated, I grab a cushion and hold it in my lap, needing something to squeeze tightly.

"Are you really okay?" I ask Rafe, and he twists his body so he's facing me, tucking one leg under himself.

"It's probably going to be a while before I'm completely okay. At Oakley House, they said there's not really a timeline for how these things go. I'll probably still have my good days and bad days but now, I know how to manage them," he tells me.

"And you're on medication too?" I ask, as he'd mentioned it before but I didn't want to pry with everyone else around.

"Antidepressants. And they're helping. It took me a couple different

132

tries to find the right one but I think this one is the best one for me, so we will see how it goes," he tells me, with a small shoulder shrug.

"You promise you'll tell us if things are getting bad again though?" I ask him, squeezing the cushion tighter.

"Definitely. If I've learnt one thing from Oakley House it's that I can't keep everything bottled in . It's alright to lean on other people," he tells me. "Now do you want to tell me what the nightmare was about?" he asks, raising one eyebrow.

I let out a long sigh, wringing my hands together because I don't want him to feel bad but he continues to stare at me, waiting ever so patiently so I cave and tell him the truth.

"It was about the night I found you in the water. They are always about that night," I confess, lowering my eyes to the couch.

"Do you have nightmares a lot?" he asks, sadly.

"Not very often now."

"I'm sorry that I caused them Petal. And I'm sorry you had to go through that for me," he says, trying to look into my eyes which I still have lowered. He puts his fist under my chin, lifting my eyes to his. "I'm not sorry that you saved me though. I will forever be grateful for that," a small smile lifts up the corner of his lips.

"I'm glad I got there in time," I tell him, with silent tears streaming down my face. He lifts me into his arms, as we bury our faces in the other's neck as he soothes my sobs.

"Thank you," he whispers, into the quiet air.

I lean back and we stare into each other's eyes. Footsteps on the stairs have me looking up to Tate with worry on his face.

"Everything okay?" he asks, as he steps closer.

"Yeah, I just had a nightmare and Rafe woke me up and then we came down here to talk," I tell him, as he takes a spot next to Rafe and holds out his arms. I move off Rafe's lap and into Tate's and rest my ear against his chest while his chin sits on the top of my head.

"You good?"

"Yeah," Rafe and I both reply, which makes us all laugh.

"I'm gonna head back to bed," Rafe says, standing up then he gives us a small smile before disappearing up the stairs. Tate's hand rubs my back as I lift my head to look into his eyes.

"You still having nightmares?" he asks .

Letting out a sigh I say, "Yeah, I think seeing Rafe again triggered another one is all," as I wrap my arms tightly around his waist, squeezing him tight.

"Hopefully knowing that he is okay will help settle them a bit," he says, trying to comfort me. "You wanna head back to bed?"

"Let's go," I say, taking his hand and walking up the stairs with him. Once in bed I snuggle up to his chest, resting my ear over his heartbeat and let the thumping beat settle my soul and soothe me to sleep.

-- Tate --

As I lie in bed with Tamsyn, her body relaxes and I know she's finally asleep. I let my thoughts wander. My first thought when I saw her in Rafe's arm was jealousy. I know they are just friends but it's still hard to not let emotions like jealousy spark when you see your girl in the arms of another guy. Even if he is one of your best friends.

I'm glad Rafe is back and seems better. Nothing could have wiped the smile off JP's face tonight and that alone was worth it. I've been worried about him since Rafe left to get help. I'll have to keep checking in with Rafe too to make sure he's doing okay. And Tamsyn too for that matter. I wish her mind would settle in her sleep. She said she hadn't had a nightmare for a while so I'm hoping they aren't resurfacing. It's the last thing she needs, especially when she is finally getting back on track at school. With my mind racing with thoughts, it takes me a while to fall back asleep but when sleep finally comes, it is a welcome break from the swirling in my head.

On Saturday we decide to go over to Penny's house for a swim since Rafe is back. Surprisingly her parents are home so we get to meet them briefly before they head out for lunch and leave us to take over the pool. Rafe's presence has lightened the mood and everyone is so much happier now that he's back. It's amazing how when one person is missing from the group that you notice their absence immensely. And then once they return it settles something, like all is right in the world again.

It's now Monday morning and we have human bio. Walking hand in hand with Tamsyn, we enter the classroom and take our seats with Scott. The rest of the students file in and fill their seats too while Ms. Chadwick is writing on the whiteboard, getting the class ready. With my eyes on the door, I see Rafe push it open and his face lights up when he catches sight of us.

"Hey guys," his loud voice booms through the class, which has Ms. Chadwick whipping around where she stands.

"Rafe?" she questions with shock, her eyes glued to the larger than life presence which is Rafe.

He turns towards her when he hears his name saying, "Hey Miss," in a quieter voice. I glance at my teacher and catch the shimmer of unshed tears glossing over her eyes before she shakes her head.

"It's nice to see you back," she tells him, smiling.

"It's nice to be back," he replies, as he gives her a knowing nod, acknowledging the unspoken words. Rafe knows his parents filled in the principal and in turn, the staff got told about Rafe's circumstances. He takes his seat next to Scott while Ms. Chadwick continues on with writing on the board. He lowers his head, eyes on his desk.

I hear Scott ask, "You okay man?" quietly.

"Yeah, it's just I didn't realise how many people were affected by me, you know? Everyone I've seen since I got back, who knows what happened, has looked just like that. Tears in their eyes like they are holding in their relief that I'm here in the flesh. Even people who don't know what happened are happy to see me," he says, his brow furrowed in thought.

"It just shows how much you were missed and are loved, man. And how many people you affect without realising it," I tell him, hoping he can see how many people's lives would have been affected if he wasn't here anymore. I don't want him to ever get to that low point again where he believes he is alone in this world.

His eyes look up to glance at Tamsyn who is looking over her notes, not paying attention to our conversation.

"I'm lucky, that's for sure," he says, and I can see in his eyes the gratefulness he has for Tamsyn for saving him that night. He doesn't look at her with desire in his eyes like I do. So it settles my little ball of jealousy I had burning in the back of my mind. Tamsyn and the guys might be close but they don't care about each other the way she and I do. The thought has me squeezing her thigh, gaining her attention.

"What was that for?" she asks, smiling.

"I love you," I whisper, kissing her cheek before Ms. Chadwick starts the lesson.

Chapter 17

-- Tamsyn --

Friday comes far too quickly and everyone has plans. Rafe has a therapy session and Penny informed me that she and JP are going on a date. She said it's still early days so they want to be sure before they say anything to the group. I don't think they have any need to hide it but each to their own I guess. Since everyone else said they are busy, Scott said he was going to stay in and do some studying. So that leaves Tate and I.

"Do you wanna come hang out at mine tonight?" I ask Tate, as I sit next to him in the car on the way home.

His smile shines my way as he replies, "That's my favourite thing to do. I'll head home and change then come straight over." Pressing a swift kiss to my temple, I can't help but smile myself.

The guys drop me off and as I enter the front door I'm greeted by my mum rushing past yelling, "Hi, bub."

"What's got you running around and so dressed up?" I ask, looking my mum up and down as I take in her black and white maxi dress and high heels.

As she's hooking an earring into her earlobe she says, "I forgot the company has an awards dinner tonight and everyone has to go. Is the gang coming over for a sleepover tonight?"

"No, everyone is busy but Tate so he's going to come hang out," I tell her, as I turn to walk up the stairs. Threading her other earring in, she follows me. She grabs her purse hanging on the stair rail, takes out some cash and hands it to me.

"Okay, can you two order some dinner then? It's a dinner and drinks thing so I will probably be late home."

"Yeah no worries Mum. You aren't driving, are you?" I ask, turning to her before I head through my open bedroom door.

"I was planning to, why?" she asks, with a raised brow.

"Why don't you catch an Uber and have some drinks Mum. Might be nice to have a night to relax you know," I tell her. Mum and Dad always used to go out for dinner and drinks once a month but since he passed the most Mum has done is go out to the movies. I haven't seen her let her hair down in all the time that's passed since his death.

"You think so?" she asks, as she bites her lower lip, considering it.

"I know so. Go have fun Mum. I'll be fine with Tate. Enjoy yourself," I tell her, which has her smile shining.

"Okay then. I'll order an Uber now," she says, walking down the hall to her bedroom. I get into my bedroom, put my bag down and place the cash on my bedside table.

She rushes back in a few minutes later as I'm getting ready to go to the shower.

"The Uber is nearly here bub, so I'm off. I'll see you later. If you need me, just give me a ring," she informs me, kissing my head as she takes off down the stairs.

"Have fun Mum," I yell after her. I hurry through my shower, trying to get finished before Tate arrives. Wrapping myself in a fluffy towel, I head to my room but am stopped by the knocking on the front door. I race down the stairs and fling it open, greeted by a smiling Tate, his recently washed hair dripping on his t-shirt. His eyes peruse me in my towel as I take a step back, letting him in.

"You caught me as I was heading to my room," I tell him, as I turn my back to him, knowing he will follow. The sound of the door closing has me looking over my shoulder, catching Tate gazing at my bare legs. His eyes meet mine with a twinkle at being caught and he quickens his steps, wrapping his arms around my waist and pulling me in close for a hug before letting go. "Mum has gone out to a work event for the night, so it's just us," I tell him, as we trek up the stairs.

"Oh really," he says, taking his usual spot on my bed. Hands behind his head, keeping his eyes trained on me. A blush creeps over my whole body as he lies there taking me in. Time stands still as we gaze at each other, my heart galloping in my chest. He finally breaks the silence, "Come here, Sweetness." With timid steps I walk next to the bed as he reaches out his hand for me to take. He pulls me to straddle his lap and I instantly become more aware of the fact I'm naked under my towel. I wriggle on his lap trying to get comfortable but Tate grabs my hips, shifting me into place.

"You're killing me Sweetness," he softly says, as I feel his hardness growing underneath me. He shifts my loose hair back over my shoulder. "Have I told you lately how beautiful you are?" he softly asks, his eyes trained on my hair he just moved.

"Not in the last ten minutes you haven't," I say giggling, which makes him smile wider.

"Cheeky now, aren't you?" he playfully taunts, as he tickles my sides

139

which has me laughing harder. I try to roll away from him to escape the torture but it's no use, he's too strong.

"Don't Tate," I laugh louder, as he continues to exploit my weakness. In my haste to get away, I end up under him as he hovers above me. As we both realise the position we are in, the laughter stops and electric energy fills the air. Tate leans forward delivering a line of kisses along my collarbone which has my breath hitching as I close my eyes. He nudges the piece of the best friend's necklace he got me with his nose. His own half of the necklace dangles from around his neck. Neither of us have taken them off since he gave it to me. His lips move slowly up my neck until they touch my own, savouring me. I wrap my arms around his neck pulling me closer. Needing more.

Losing ourselves in the kiss, he whips his t-shirt off one handed. Granting me access to his bare chest, I lower my hands rubbing it over his smooth skin, which ignites a masculine groan from him. As I stare into his eyes I realise I don't want to wait anymore. I'm ready to be with Tate.

"I don't wanna wait anymore," I tell him, which has him freezing on top of me.

"Are you sure?" he asks, searching my eyes for answers. I nod in reply.

"I'm ready," I tell him, as I unhook my towel letting it unravel, exposing my naked body to him fully. His eyes soak every inch of me in as he leans back on his heels.

"Hold on," he says, as he hops off the bed making me question what he's doing. He walks to my bedroom door, and before I can cover myself he closes the door and turns to me with a shy smile. "It felt weird with the door open," he says, shrugging his shoulders as he comes back to me. He unzips his jeans and peels them off, so he stands before me in his red boxers. Never once letting his eyes leave mine. I lift my hips and pull the towel free, letting it fall to the floor. I watch his adam's apple as he visibly gulps, before sliding back on top of me.

140

Chapter 17

"We can stop at any time, just tell me, okay?" he says, sweetly.

"Okay," I reply, as I cup his cheek. One side of his lips lift with a lopsided smile as he starts trailing kisses down my neck towards my breasts, taking first one nipple into his mouth then the other. Moving further south his gentle kisses brush the skin of my stomach as his body moves backwards until he's dragging me to the end of the bed which has me laughing. "Tate?" I question, with a giggle in my voice unsure what he's up to. I lean up on my forearms staring at him as he kneels on the floor. "What are you doing?" I ask.

"You trust me?" he asks, holding my gaze.

"Yeah," I reply.

"You ever had anyone go down on you before?" he asks, and I can feel my cheeks heat as I shake my head.

"Have you ever done it before?" I ask him, and his own cheeks darken as she shakes his head.

"I want to now though," he tells me. I push my self conscious thoughts aside and nod wanting to experience this with him. "Just relax," he says, as he gently pushes my knees apart. He grabs my butt cheeks and pulls me right to the end of the bed. "Every inch of you is beautiful," I barely hear him say, as I lie my head back down.

All my senses are on high alert as the anticipation builds up. I feel his warm breath on my inner thigh as he delivers a kiss to one leg and then the other. His fingers open me up and then his firm tongue swipes my whole center. My head is thrown back against the bed from the feeling. His tongue licks at my sensitive bud, causing more sensations to flood through me as I release a moan. I vaguely register a chuckle from him as he continues his movements with his tongue.

"Can I put a finger in?" he asks.

I all but yell, "Yes," in reply as my body takes over my thoughts. As his finger penetrates my body, my hips buckle against the sensations as his tongue continues devouring me. Moving his finger in and out he slowly adds a second, stretching me. I feel the pulsing start in my lower belly and before I know it, I'm exploding with quiet moans as my body shakes. I peek down at him, my body relaxed as his grinning face comes into view.

"Good?" he asks, and I can't help my own smile.

"Amazing," I tell him, as he crawls back on top of me. He kisses me and I taste myself on him and it drives me to kiss him deeper, knowing we shared something so intimate. "Get a condom out of the bedside table," I tell him, breaking the kiss.

"You're sure? We can stop if you want," he tells me.

"I'm sure. I want you Tate. All of you," he smiles, kissing my forehead before getting up. He rustles around in the brown bag of condoms pulling one out. He pulls his boxers all the way down and my eyes zone in on the sight of him. It's my turn to gulp at his hard length. I'm not sure how it's all supposed to fit inside me.

He must read my mind because he says, "If most people in the world are doing it, it's gotta fit, right?" and I can't help but laugh. He always knows what to say to calm my thoughts. "Do you wanna help with this?" he asks, holding up the condom between two fingers. I sit up and grab it as he takes a seat next to me. I rip it open and together we figure out the right way for it to go on and then lower it down. He hisses out of his lips, eyes closed and I get lost in watching how my touch affects him.

We move back with me lying under him again and get lost in kissing each other. He swipes his fingers across my nipples so I do the same to him, making his kisses greedier.

He breaks the kiss, "You ready?" he asks, and I nod. I widen my legs as he lines himself up with my centre. He slowly eases himself in and I watch as his eyes close, his breathing speeds up. Feeling full, he keeps going until I feel a burn and my body stiffens. His eyes open, looking at me. "You okay?" he asks.

"Yeah it just burns, but it's what I've been told to expect. Keep going and kiss me," I tell him, which has his lips touching mine as he pushes further in, the burn intensifying. I release his mouth, steadying my breaths as I adjust to him being inside me. He holds himself still with his forehead pressed to mine. "Move," I tell him. His eyes stare into mine as he slides himself out and then back in. The burn has lessened and feels better the more he moves.

"You feel so good, Sweetness, I don't think I'll last much longer," he tells me.

"That's okay. Let go," I tell him, as I cup his cheek again. "I love you," I whisper.

"I love you too, baby," he replies, kissing my lips as his movements quicken and then he drops his head into the crook of my neck as his groans fill the air, his body shuddering. The sounds of our erratic breathing fill the air as we stay still. He shifts himself to look into my eyes with a lazy smile on his lips. "You okay?" he asks.

"I'm perfect," I tell him. Delivering a chaste kiss to my lips, he slowly pulls himself out of me and I feel the loss of him. He removes the condom and ties it off before dropping it to the floor. He pulls me into his chest and holds me close.

"How are you feeling?" he asks me, and I have to think for a second to get my thoughts in order.

"It's weird. I feel the same but different all at the same time," I tell him, as my shaking hand runs down his chest. He notices the shake and grabs my hand, frowning.

"I didn't hurt you, did I? Why are you shaking?" he asks, worry lacing his voice as he searches my eyes.

"I think it's just the shock of not being a virgin anymore. It's a big thing, you know?" I tell him, because I don't know how else to explain it.

"I don't want you thinking it wasn't amazing because it was," I tell him, knowing without a doubt I wouldn't have changed a thing.

"I'm glad I waited for my green fairy," he sweetly tells me, and I smile up at him feeling a full heart.

"I'm glad I waited for you too," I tell him, which has a bright smile lighting up his face. My shaking hands finally stop the longer I stay wrapped in his embrace.

-- Tate --

"How about we go have a shower after I order some pizza?" I ask her, which she agrees with.

I quickly ring and order pizza before I pick her up in my arms, carrying her laughing into the bathroom. With her legs wrapped tightly around my naked body, I can't help but feel I never want to be without this girl. We've been through so much to get here. I want to continue on this way forever.

I feel so satisfied after having sex and it felt a million times better than getting off with my hand. It's like a piece of me has been taken by this wonderful girl and I don't ever want it back if I get to keep the memory of what just happened with me forever. I turn the shower on and when it's warmed up, I push us both under the spray.

I push her wet hair out of her smiling face, and take her lips with mine, letting the water run over both of us. After a while, I place her on her feet and pump some body wash into my hands before smoothing it all over her. She does the same to me and I can't help the obvious hardening of my erection her touch causes.

"Just ignore him," I tell her, as her eyes gaze at me and we both laugh. I finish cleaning myself and she does the same. I notice she winces as she runs body wash over herself.

144

"You alright?" I ask, worried.

"Yeah, just stings a bit is all." I gather her close as she rests her head on my chest.

After a few minutes of standing there in each other's embrace I say, "Come on we better go, pizza will be here soon." I grab towels for us both and we dry off then head back to the room. Tamsyn puts on a tank top and sleep shorts while I put my boxers back on.

"I better put this in the bin. It would've been awkward if Mum walked in and saw it," she says, holding up the condom and wrapper we left on the floor for anyone to see. My smile beams at her while she hides the evidence in the rubbish bin. My gaze moves to the dishevelled sheets and I notice a spot of blood on them.

"Sweetness, are you sure you're okay? Look," I say, pointing at the evidence on her bed which has her cheeks turning pink.

"That's quite normal. A lot of girls bleed their first time," she tells me. "Can you help me change them?" she asks, and she throws the duvet on the floor and starts unhooking the fitted sheet to change. I jump into action and start pulling it off with her then she takes it to the laundry and returns with a clean sheet, which we put on together. The knocking on the front door has me running down the stairs to get the pizza, which I meet her in the kitchen with.

"You know what, how about we just take the food up in the box and eat in bed?" she suggests, so I grab some soda cans out of the fridge and follow her while she carries the food. Getting comfortable on the bed, we flick a movie on and dive into the pizza, both of us having gained an appetite from our workout.

She's quiet while we eat and is lost in her thoughts which makes me nervous.

"You don't regret it, do you Sweetness?" I quietly ask her, my gaze suddenly interested in the duvet. She pushes the pizza box out of the way and crawls into my lap, wrapping her arm and legs tightly around me.

"Of course I don't regret it. Sorry I'm so quiet, I'm just lost in my head is all," she tells me.

"Do you want to talk about it?" I ask.

Her face darkens before she says, "Do you think anyone is going to be able to tell we aren't virgins anymore?" and I can't help but chuckle.

"I doubt it. Can you tell who has had sex and who hasn't just by looking at them?" I ask, trying to lighten the mood which makes her smile.

"No I guess not," she concedes.

"So nothing to worry about. Just don't be jumping my bones every minute of every day and no one will know," I say, laughing louder as she playfully swats at my chest.

"I see you think very highly of yourself, don't you?" she taunts.

"Well next time I'll last longer," I tell her, staring into her eyes.

"I didn't even notice how long it was. It was perfect to me," she softly says, kissing my lips which makes my heart sigh. I was worried I had finished too fast as it felt so good inside her I couldn't hold back any longer. I quickly kiss her forehead then move her to snuggle into my chest as we watch the movie. I double check the door is wide open so her mum doesn't get suspicious when she gets home and then relax. Before I know it, I'm drifting off to sleep, feeling a peace I haven't felt for a long time.

Chapter 18

-- Tamsyn --

The week for camp rolls around and everyone is buzzing with excitement. A whole week off school and getting to do fun activities sounds like bliss. Everyone had to be at school by seven thirty to pile into the buses and head the few hours to our destination. The camping resort we are going to is the same one all the seniors in past years have gone to. Camp Stargaze is what it's called. It sounds like fate to me. As all the seniors squeeze onto the two yellow buses, I sit with Tate while JP, Rafe, Scott and Penny sit in a four seater in front of us. The chatter and laughter fills the air as everyone settles in for the ride.

Nearly three hours and one pit stop later and we pull up to an isolated location in between hills and paddocks. The buses bump along the dusty road leading to a series of white buildings with red roofs. Parking up in front of the main building, Mr Finnegan, who is in charge of our bus, instructs us on what to do.

"Okay kids, we are going to hop off the bus and gather with the rest of the seniors. The camp director has a few words they want to share before you can grab your bags and find a room."

As we all stand to make our way out of the bus, the mid morning sun hits us with its heat. I'm thankful I decided to wear a singlet and shorts even though it was chilly this morning when we left. Tate tugs on my hand leading me to where the others stand, as we wait for more instructions.

A tall older man with an orange scraggly beard and a brown wide brimmed hat stands before us. His eyes are covered with thick black sunglasses but he removes them before addressing us.

"Welcome to Camp Stargaze everyone. The team and I here are so happy you could join us for the week," he cheerily says, gesturing to the rest of the staff behind him. "I'm your camp director Mr Reynolds. You can call me Sir or even Steve will do. We aren't too formal around here. During your stay, you'll learn the rest of the names of the staff. The only thing we ask is you treat us with respect and in turn, we will do the same to you." He stares at all of us, gauging our reactions. I wonder if he's trying to find the troublemakers of the group.

Once he's satisfied no one is going to chip in with any smart remarks he continues, "Our cabins have four beds each, two sets of bunk beds. We have one area for girls and one for boys. There will be no mingling and sneaking around at night as the staff and teachers will be monitoring the areas. Your teachers have split you up into smaller groups for activities. Some activities will be in these smaller groups and some activities can accommodate the entire group. So with that, you can grab your bags and go in search of a cabin. Boys you are towards the right and girls are to the left. Drop your bags off and then we will meet back here at our main site for lunch."

As he finishes, murmurs begin and everyone heads to the buses in search of their bags.

Tate keeps a firm grip of my hand as he leans down to my ear, "Sucks we can't be in the same cabin," he whispers, before his lips meet the skin behind my ear, sending a shiver through my body. Since we had sex, we haven't found a moment alone together to do it again. I talked to my mum the day after and told her what happened. She was worried like any good mother would be but is glad we were safe and the experience was a good one.

To say things are heated between Tate and I would be an understatement. I don't think anyone else in the group knows we had sex but we find more ways to touch each other lately, and our gazes linger a bit longer too. Tate pulls me out of my daydreaming and towards the bus where he grabs both our bags, handing me mine.

"I'll see you at lunch," he says, and I nod as he leaves to walk in the opposite direction with Rafe, Scott and JP.

Penny and I watch them leave. We both let out a sigh then look at each other and crack up laughing. She links her arm through mine and we head towards the cabins on the left.

"The guys are lucky there are four of them. They can get a cabin together," Penny says.

"Oh man, I didn't even think of that. Let's hurry and hope we get a good one." We pick up the pace, power walking past a few groups of girls who are taking their time laughing on their way to the cabins. As we reach them, we notice the cabins are in a long rectangular building with doors scattered all the way down. Ms. Chadwick greets us as we get there.

"Just choose a room, ladies. Leave your bag on your bed so other girls know it's taken and then we can head back for lunch. Only four to a cabin," she tells us. Penny and I start our hunt but find the first few are already full so we keep looking, until we come to one of the last ones which is empty.

"Yes, let's take this one," Penny says, entering the small room with bunk beds on either side of the walls.

"Do you want the top? I can sleep on the bottom so at least if someone joins us, we are still on the same side," Penny suggests.

"Sounds good," I say, swinging my bag and pillow up onto the top bunk. Climbing up to the top bunk, I lie down to test out the bed while Penny does the same to hers and we both laugh and talk about how much fun this week will be. "Tate and I had sex," I blurt, while my face heats as her head pops out from her bed, looking at me with an open mouth.

"What? Oh my God, when?" she asks, shock written across her face.

"Only a couple weeks ago," I tell her, wringing my hands.

"And you're just telling me now?" she accuses, with a smile spreading across her face.

"I haven't really had time alone with you and I didn't want to blurt it over the lunch table in front of the guys," I say, which has us both laughing. She climbs up the ladder and takes a seat on my bed with me.

"So how was it?" she asks.

"Perfect. Honestly I'm so glad it was with Tate," I tell her.

"Yeah you're lucky. My first time was in the back of this guy Colin's car and most of our clothes were still on," she says as her face scrunches up thinking of the memory. Shaking herself out of her head she asks, "Did it hurt?"

"Yeah, I knew it would but jeez that burns like crazy," I tell her, and we both start cracking up.

Our laughter gets interrupted by Leyla and Chloe entering the room. Penny gives them the evil eye and they both visibly cringe.

"Sorry we will find somewhere else," Chloe says.

"But I don't wanna be split up," Leyla tries to whisper to Chloe, but I hear her.

"Are all the other cabins pretty full?" I ask, my eyes flicking between the two of them.

"Yeah, most only have one spot in each room left. Would it be okay if we stayed in here? We'll keep out of your way."

Leyla pleads and before Penny can deny them I say, "Yeah, that's fine," which has Penny staring at me with raised brows.

"Oh my gosh, thanks so much," Leyla gushes, while Chloe smiles wide. They each take a bed opposite us with Leyla on the top bunk. Penny and I decide to leave for lunch but before we leave Leyla grabs my arm. "Thanks for this Tam, it really means a lot," she says.

"It's no problem. I never thanked you for contacting Tate about my birthday so call us even," I say, smiling at her.

"Sure," she says, and we leave them to it.

"Are you sure you're alright with sharing a room with them?" Penny questions, when we are out of earshot.

"Yeah, it'll be fine. I haven't had much to do with them since Blake and my issue is more with him now than them. Plus Leyla did apologise for it all."

"Okay, as long as you're sure," Penny tells me, linking her arm back with mine.

"Yeah, I'm tired of holding onto anger towards them. Anyway if I didn't have the fall out with them, I wouldn't have become friends with you," I tell her, meaning every word. I may not have been friends with Penny as long as Leyla and Chloe but she's been a better friend in every way.

"And I'm extremely grateful we became friends," she says, leaning her head on my shoulder.

"Don't worry, this week will be fun no matter what," I tell her, as we follow other kids into the lunch hall in search of the guys. Of course they are already seated, shovelling large amounts of food into their mouths. I honestly don't think they ever get full with the way they gobble every meal. Penny and I grab a tray each and pile on some sandwiches and fruit before walking over to where the guys sit. I sit next to Tate while Penny sits herself opposite me, next to JP.

"Hey you," Tate says, between mouthfuls of food.

"Hey yourself," I say, as I take a bite of my own sandwich.

"Did you girls get a good cabin?" Rafe asks, on the other side of Tate.

"Yeah, but Leyla and Chloe are bunking with us," Penny tells the table, which has all eyes on me.

"I'm okay guys. Hopefully I won't be in the same group as them so I'll only see them when sleeping, which won't be that bad," I tell them. "You guys all together?" I ask.

"Yeah, JP and I on one side and Tate and Scott on the other," Rafe tells me. I offer Rafe a small smile which he returns. It's nice to have him with us on this trip after everything that's happened. He's still the same Rafe, just less outspoken than he was beforehand.

After lunch, the teachers announce the groups and luckily all of us are together which is the best thing that could have happened. I want my memories of this camp to contain my friends. Our first activity is kayaking so we get suited up with life jackets and then hop into a van with Mr. Finnegan and one of the camp staff Mr. Arrow.

It's about a ten minute drive and then we are pulling up to a wide blue lake. There are already kayaks lined up on the grass in front of the water so we jump out and pair up. Our group is pretty good. It is the six of us then JP's friend Elijah, another guy Tyler, his girlfriend Hope and her friend Valerie. Tate and I pair up together and he tells me to hop in while he pulls it out into the lake a bit before he jumps in himself.

The sounds of laughter fill the breeze as we all paddle around the lake, trying not to bump into each other. It isn't long before we have our first casualties when Hope and Valerie find their kayak tipped over. While they wade in the water we all laugh at their misfortune but then I catch Rafe tipping JP and Penny's kayak. It makes me wonder if he tipped the girls too. It's nice to see him up to his old tricks.

"Keep away from Rafe, he's tipping them," I yell to Tate, who starts paddling away from Rafe and Scott. We spend the rest of the time keeping away from Rafe who manages to flip Elijah and Tyler's kayak before it's time to go back in. Mr, Finnegan doesn't look impressed with the ones who look like drowned rats. He must have missed the part where Rafe gave them a helping hand. Mr Arrow comes out of the little office-like structure they have and hands the wet kids towels to dry off.

When we get back to the main campsite kids are rushing around and Rafe yells out, "Hey, where's the fire?" to one of the other guys from our year.

"They've made up water slides with some plastic and dish soap over on the hill," he yells back, as he takes off in the direction of the slides. We all exchange glances, coming to the same conclusion.

"Let's get changed and meet at the slides," JP yells, as he and Rafe take off with Scott and Tate, hot on their heels. Penny and I quickly make our way to our cabin and get changed into our swimsuits, singlets and board shorts before we rush over to the hill where all the commotion is coming from.

As it comes into view, it looks like most of the kids are here, running up the hill and sliding down the bubbly slick surface. Rafe comes barrelling down with the biggest smile I've seen on his face in a long time and it makes something settle inside my soul to see him so happy again.

"Come on slow pokes, get moving," he teases Penny and I, as he pushes us up the hill to get in line. As we rush up, Scott comes sliding down past us with a matching smile to Rafe's. Since nearly all of the kids are out here, they are setting up a third slide so we aren't all waiting too long for a turn. When we reach the top, JP flies down the plastic and Tate pulls both Penny and I in front of him, letting us cut in line. Penny doesn't wait, throwing herself down with a giggle as she goes.

"Your turn," Tate says, pulling my back into his chest quickly before releasing me. I lower myself to the wet plastic which is surprisingly heated from the sun. Using my hands, I launch myself forward, remembering at the last second to keep my mouth closed so it doesn't get dish soap water in it. I can't help the squeal that exits half way down when I realise how fast I'm going. Penny's face lights up when I reach the bottom, pulling me up. I turn in time to see Tate launch himself down, his own smile blinding me as he slides down, greeting me at the end.

"Come on, let's go again," Penny urges, as she races up the hill and Tate and I follow behind, hand in hand. They've got the third slide set up now so the lines are shorter. That's how we spend the rest of the afternoon before the teachers come out to collect everyone for showers and dinner.

After dinner, everyone disperses to their own cabins for the night. They haven't planned anything for our first night since they wanted us to settle in. I give Tate a kiss goodbye and when Penny and I arrive at the cabin, Leyla and Chloe are already in there, getting changed for bed. I pull out my own pajamas from my bag and quickly change, trying not to be too self conscious.

"Hey Tam," Chloe says, from her spot on her bed behind me.

"Hey."

"You look a lot healthier now," she says cringing. "Ugh, that didn't come out right. I mean you look happier now and your weight looks better on you. I know I envied it before but that was before I realised you weren't eating properly because of your dad."

Chapter 18

"That doesn't sound much better Chlo," Leyla says.

"Ugh, you know what I mean, don't you Tam? I'm happy that you're happy," she explains. I offer her a small smile.

"Thanks Chloe, yeah I am happy," I tell her, as I climb into my own bed. We lie in the dark in silence, none of us knowing what to say.

"Miss Dermot, where do you think you are sneaking off to with that flash light? Get back to your cabin before I confiscate it," we hear Ms. Chadwick yell, which has us all cracking up with laughter, breaking the tension.

"Oh my gosh, she must have been sneaking off to see Drew. I saw them making out by the showers while everyone else was up on the water slides," Chloe says, filling us in.

"No way, I thought she was seeing Derrick?" Penny asks, astonished.

"That's what I thought too. Derrick probably doesn't know," Chloe says.

"Well we know one thing for sure, she does like her D," Leyla giggles, and it has us all howling with laughter before Ms. Chadwick bangs on our door, telling us to go to sleep which has us giggling behind covered mouths, trying to keep the noise contained.

"Miss has a long night ahead of her," Penny says, which has us all trying to contain our laughter some more. As our laughter dies, we all say our goodnights and try to sleep.

Don't Fade. Breathe Easy.

Chapter 19

-- Tate --

We wake up early Tuesday morning and after brushing our teeth and getting changed, we follow the other students to the dining hall for breakfast. As we enter, my eyes automatically search for Tamsyn. I find her and Penny in the spot we were in yesterday. With a bright smile plastered on my face, I go over and say hi before grabbing a tray and filling it with cereal and toast and my much needed caffeine.

"Does anyone know what our group is doing today?" JP asks, as he slides into the seat next to Penny. I do the same next to Tamsyn and she turns to me, her eyes lighting up as she smiles.

"I think it'll probably either be abseiling or the high ropes course," Scott says, from his spot across from me. That starts the others talking while I squeeze Tamsyn's thigh under the table. I lean in closer to whisper so only she will hear.

"I missed you last night," I tell her, honestly. It was hard to fall asleep in a strange bed even though I was surrounded by the guys.

"I missed you too," she replies. "Hopefully we get some free time today and can spend some together." My heart races at the thought. I want nothing more than to spend some time alone with her. I inch my hand up higher on her thigh which has her breath hitching as she tries to not draw attention to us from the others. They are too distracted with talk of the high ropes to notice us anyway. She's wearing tight jean shorts so my movements get halted by her clothes as I can't go any further up. Instead I run my fingers up and down her leg and watch as her cheeks change colour.

All too soon the others are clearing their plates so I reluctantly follow suit, giving Tamsyn a cheeky grin meant for her eyes only. We meet the rest of our group out the front of the dining hall with an instructor called Jack.

"Hey everyone, so today you are with me and we are abseiling," he tells us, which starts the excitement back up again. "The rest of my team is already at the tower so we are going to walk through the forest track to get to our climbing spot. Everyone follow me." We all fall in line, following behind him as everyone talks about how much fun this is going to be. I squeeze Tamsyn's hand as we walk, running my thumb back and forth.

"You aren't afraid of heights, are you?" I ask her, unsure.

"Ha ha ha I live for danger," she fake laughs at me, which has us both cracking up. Once our outburst is under control she says, "Nah, I don't think so. It's not like I go out of my way to be around heights or anything though so who knows," which has me holding her hand tighter.

The further we walk into the forest track, the more the sun disappears, leaving us in a dim lit area, which gives me an idea.

"You know, this would be a good place to hide," I whisper to her, which has her gazing up at me, reading my thoughts.

"Later?" she asks.

"Later," I say.

After about a ten minute walk, we arrive at an open field with a high wooden square structure. The other instructors come to greet us and we get into practice abseiling. They teach us all to belay and about harnesses. We spend the morning going over all the safety aspects and what we need to do. Lunch rolls around and we make our way back to eat before we come back to the tower to start the fun part of the day.

The group gets split in half. One half will go up while the other half stay on the ground, watching what the instructors do for the belaying. We aren't going to belay ourselves but we are going to call out to the people abseiling, as if we were so we get the full experience.

The girls plus Elijah are in the first group. Tamsyn looks cute in her orange helmet and I can tell from the look on her face she's nervous. They all get clipped onto a line as they go into the structure to take the stairs, leading up to the first station. As you look up at it from the ground, it looks surprisingly high. I'd hate to think what it will look like from their angle.

Elijah is up first and he makes it look easy. He bounces down the wall as the instructor has to rush to get down before him. Next up is Valerie and her screams reach our ears before she's even over the edge.

"I guess someone might have a fear of heights," JP says, as we all look up. She's on the edge and her screams fill the air. She drops a little and starts to freak out. The instructor is right under her as he helps bring her down to the ground slowly. Once she's safe on solid ground, she lays down. I don't think she'll be doing that again. Scott goes over to sit by her to see if she's okay.

"Tamsyn's up bro," JP says, and I follow his gaze up towards where she's about to step over the side.

"You got this Sweetness," I yell up to her, not caring what anyone thinks. She descends like a pro even bouncing off the wall a few times, closer to the bottom. As her feet hit the ground, I can't help staring at the mesmerising smile taking over her whole face. Her eyes catch mine and once she's unhooked, she runs to me and I pull her into my arms.

"That was awesome," she squeals into my chest, her excitement rubbing off on me. The guys all smile at her enthusiasm too. We all watch as Penny abseils down in a similar fashion as if she's been doing it for years and not hours. I can tell from JP's wide eyed expression he's impressed. Hope is the last one from their group and once she's done, it's our turn to trade places and go up.

When we reach the spot where we are going to drop from, there are seats lining the back wall so we all sit down, waiting for our turn. Rafe is up first and is bouncing on the balls of his feet with nervous energy. He listens to the instructor intently and then moves into the spot to lower himself. He gives us a wink as he disappears over the side.

"See you on the other side," he yells back to us, making us all chuckle.

JP is up next and then Scott follows him. When it's my turn, I wipe my sweaty hands on my shorts before putting on my gloves and listening to the instructor. As I take my place and lean back, a shot of adrenaline races through me as I drop slightly. Letting out some of the rope, I start descending. I use my feet to push off from the wall, testing it at first and then gaining more confidence, I jump further out, enjoying my time on the wall. Planting my feet on the ground, I'm sure I've got the silly excited grin on my face to match everyone else minus Valerie.

Tyler is the last to take his turn and once he's finished Jack says, "So that was great. You all did a good job listening to the instructors and doing what you needed to. Now who wants to take a shot from right at the top?" pointing all the way to the highest point of the structure.

Everyone is buzzing off the first abseil so everyone except Valerie and Hope agree to go up to the top. We all take our turns and it's a lot more exhilarating abseiling from an even higher height. The atmosphere and adrenaline follows us as we finish up and head back to the dining hall. It's not quite dinner time so we get a bit of time to ourselves. So I take my opportunity to be alone with Tamsyn, dragging her back into the forest while the others are too distracted by today's activity to notice us missing.

Hand in hand, our feet hitting the dusty path, we delve further into the forest, following a different track not knowing where it's leading. Our laughter follows us the deeper we go until we come to a thick oak tree and I pull Tamsyn behind it, hiding her from view of anyone coming down the path. Smiling at her, I push her back gently into the tree, lowering my lips to hers and letting my body take over. It has a mind of its own today.

Her delicate hands wrap around my neck, pulling my body flush against her. When she feels my hardness digging into her stomach, she gasps and I swallow it down, running my fingers down her sides. A hunger for each other takes over until we are clawing at each other because we can't get enough. I have to pull away in case someone happens to come down the path and catches us.

Our pants fill the air as I rest my forehead on hers, briefly closing my eyes.

"You've got me wanting to risk sneaking out to find you tonight," I tell her, honestly.

"I think you'll have a hard time getting past Ms. Chadwick, she was on patrol most of last night," she tells me, gasping as she tries to catch her breath.

"We'll just have to make the most of our stolen secret moments then, won't we?" I say, leaning in to take her lips again. We get lost in the moment, too caught up in each other. I barely hear the breaking of a tree branch followed by voices.

I pull away from Tamsyn, hold my finger to my lips to shush as we listen.

"I tell you, the girls can't be as bad as the boys. I caught two of them trying to sneak out last night and I had to confiscate fireworks off Mr Jeffers," Mr. Finnegan complains, as footsteps become closer.

"I caught Miss Dermot trying to escape with a flashlight and half of the cabins were filled with laughter until the early hours this morning. I'm gonna hardly get any sleep this week," Ms. Chadwick's voice rings out. I tug Tamsyn's hand to pull her around the opposite side of the tree before they catch us as they walk down our path.

"At least we aren't on duty tonight. How about we have a nightcap after dinner tonight?" Mr. Finnegan suggests, as we creep further around the tree base out of view, hiding on the opposite side as they continue on their way, unaware.

"That would be great," we hear Ms. Chadwick reply, before their voices fade into the distance. We cover our mouths to hold in our laughter before I peek to check the coast is clear. Then I tug Tamsyn's hand and we race back up the path the way we came, releasing our laughter once we are out of the forest and back in the sunlight.

"Oh man, how close was that?" I say, catching my breath as we head back towards the dining hall for dinner.

"Too close," Tamsyn agrees. Entering the hall we see most of the students have already settled in to eat their dinner so we load up plates and take seats by the others.

"Where did you two sneak off to?" Scott asks, as we sit down.

"We were just around," Tamsyn tells him, a light pink colouring her cheeks.

"Man, you guys missed out on the flying fox. It's so cool. We can go there again after dinner if you wanna see?" Rafe enthusiastically tells us.

"Yeah sure, sounds great," I tell him.

Chapter 20
~

-- Tamsyn --

O n Wednesday, we get divided into two buses and are driven about half an hour away from camp to go to an aquatic park. It's jam packed with slides, different temperature pools and rides. The day disappears in the blink of an eye as we have free choice, so our small group spends the day racing from ride to ride. On our way back to camp, I can feel the heat of my sunburn warming my skin as I rest my head on Tate's shoulder. Ms. Chadwick shuffles to the front of the bus holding onto the backs of seats to keep her balance.

Turning to address us she says, "Okay everyone, once we get back to camp you are to quickly shower and then gather at the dining hall for dinner. After that make sure you are wearing warm clothes as we are meeting over on the west side of the camp for a campfire and to look at the stars." Cheering erupts all over the bus. I glance up at Tate and his sweet smile shines down on me.

His thumb swipes across my cheekbone, "Time under the stars with you sounds perfect," he says, and I can't help the rapid beating of my heart.

"Any time with you is perfect," I softly reply, which has his lips lifting higher before he leans forward, delivering a chaste kiss to my lips.

As soon as the bus stops, it's a chaotic scramble to race to the showers first. Everyone sprints in opposite directions. Boys one way and girls the other. Laughter fills the air as we all dodge out of each other's way. I catch up to Penny as we reach our cabin and quickly grab our shower things. Unfortunately by the time we get to the shower block, they are already occupied so we have to wait our turn.

I change into a hoodie and track pants after I'm finished in the shower, then join everyone at the dining hall. The guys are already there with newly washed hair.

"Gosh, you guys were fast," Penny says.

"Guys don't take as long in the shower as girls. I don't know what you guys get up to in there," Rafe teases, winking at us. I send a smile his way, happy Rafe's playful side has come back. He seemed low when he first arrived back from Oakley house but is looking more like his old self, the more time goes on.

As soon as everyone has filled themselves with dinner, the excited atmosphere follows us as we hike to the west side of camp. The closer we get, the better we can see a big fire pit set up surrounded by rocks to keep it contained. Some of the kids are already seated around, huddled in groups, chatting and laughing. We find a space on the far side of the fire pit where we can all sit together in our own huddled group. Tate sits behind me with his knees bent and pulls me down to sit between his legs. Wrapping his arms around me, he pulls my back against his chest and I relax into his embrace.

"It shouldn't be too much longer until it's dark out," Scott says, his gaze focused up at the darkening sky.

Elijah and Tyler walk around the fire pit to the different groups, handing out sticks and bags of marshmallows for roasting. Elijah hands our bag to Rafe and as soon as it's in his hands he opens it, stuffing a few into his mouth.

"Rafe," I squeal at him, trying not to laugh.

"Aww you know me Petal," he says, shrugging.

"Yeah yeah, your metabolism, blah blah," I reply, and we all crack up because it's always the same excuse Rafe uses to gorge on food.

"Here," he says, holding out a stick with two marshmallows already skewered on it.

"Thanks," I say, but before I can grab it, Tate takes it and leaps up walking over to the fire to toast them.

"Damn it," we hear his cuss a minute later. He's blowing out the marshmallows because they have caught on fire. I hide my giggle behind my hand.

"You're not supposed to put it right into the flames," JP tells him, holding his own laughter back.

"How would I know. I've never done it before," Tate replies, walking back with his now charred marshmallows. He takes his seat back behind me and holds the stick out in front of me.

"You wanna try one, Sweetness?" he asks, hopeful. I stare at the charcoaled marshmallow with no remaining white colour and carefully pick at a bit with my finger tips. The gooey mess comes away, feeling quite hot but I quickly put it in my mouth before I can change my mind. As the sugar substance dissolves in my mouth, I can't help but think it tastes similar to when you burn toast.

"It's not too bad," I tell Tate, and he rewards me with a kiss behind my ear, sending tingles through my body.

"Thanks baby," he whispers. I settle into Tate's back as the others get up, taking turns roasting marshmallows. Rafe comes over shortly after and hands me a stick with two golden coloured marshmallows,

"Enjoy," he says, with a cheeky smile, knowing his marshmallows look pretty close to perfect.

"Show off," Tate grumbles behind me, and I have to stifle my laughter. I pull a bit off one and can't help notice the contrast to Tate's burnt marshmallow.

"I prefer the charcoaled one, I think," I say, teasing.

"You do, do you?" Tate says into my ear, before he starts tickling my sides making me squeal. I squirm in his arms trying to move away from the torture he's inflicting. I wriggle so much I end up with my head across his leg, staring up into his sparkling eyes. His eyes turn from mischievous to lustful in a second as they flick to my lips then back to my eyes. When I see the intent in his eyes I lean up to meet his lips, tasting the stickiness from his own marshmallow on his lips.

When we break the contact I stare into his eyes and can't help but feel we are both wishing we were alone right now. I wriggle back into my original position and know Tate is thinking the same thing, if his stiffness digging into my back is anything to go by. I stifle my giggle as I wriggle against him. He grabs my hips, holding me still. I may have taken it a bit far.

"You think that's funny, do you?" Tate whispers, so only I can hear. I lean my head back against his chest, looking up into his eyes, giving him an innocent smile. "I always knew you were trouble," he says, and we both laugh so loud the others look at us. They've grown accustomed to me and Tate's secret conversations; they usually ignore them. Something which I'm grateful for.

Soft music fills the night air as the sky darkens. The twinkles of stars up above start to shine. My breath catches as I look up. It never ceases to amaze me how beautiful the stars can be. Out here, away from the city, the sky's the fullest I've ever seen it.

"So beautiful," I hear Tate say, so I glance at his face but his eyes are on me, not the sky. "The stars are pretty beautiful too," he says, winking at me and moving his chin to rest by my cheek. He squeezes me closer in his arms and we all get lost in admiring the beauty above us. "We will always have the stars, Sweetness," he whispers, so I barely hear him. But I can't help but think how true his words are. The stars have always connected us and in this moment I think they always will. The stars will always be there and I hope the same holds true for me and Tate's relationship.

-- Tate --

The remaining days at camp are so loaded with activities I barely manage a spare moment alone with Tamsyn except to steal kisses from her in between activities. We completed the high ropes course on Thursday and the entire time, I was flooded with thoughts of Quinn. It is exactly the type of adrenaline rush she would have loved. Standing up at the top of the course before starting, I had to take a deep breath before my first move. This time instead of dwelling on the fact she wasn't here for this, I made a promise to her in my head. I promised to live life to the fullest, and give more new things a go especially more things I know she would have enjoyed, like this high ropes course. I made a vow to live for her, as well as myself. It helped centre me and for the first time in so long, the thought of her wasn't accompanied by the horrible feeling of a panic attack. Maybe it's possible to still grieve for her but have my thoughts of her not burden me so much either.

In the early hours of Friday morning I'm woken up and for a brief moment I'm confused, before I remember I'm at camp. Groaning from the opposite bunks pulls my attention. In the dim lighting I can make out Rafe, thrashing around in his blankets. Without hesitation, I jump down from my side as quietly as I can and climb on the ladder. His hands are clawing at his throat so I shake him firmly to try and wake him.

"Rafe," I whisper yell, to try to wake him up without waking Scott and JP in the process. "Rafe," I say a little louder, which has his body relaxing as he wakes up in a fogginess.

"Tate?" he says unsure, looking at my face next to him.

"You okay? You were having a nightmare," I tell him. He touches his throat like he knew he was clawing at it. He's left a scratch which makes him hiss as his finger runs over the shallow wound. "Lets go to the bathroom and have a look man," I tell him, hopping down hoping he will follow, which he does.

The snores of the other two fill the small cabin so we creep to the door, slowly turning the handle. I peek my head outside to check for any teachers but when I see the coast is clear, I gesture for Rafe to follow me. We quietly sneak to the bathrooms, situated down the end of the footpath. The lights are always on in here so at least we don't need to worry about someone noticing us turn them on.

Rafe steps in front of the mirror, surveying his throat.

"Ugh, I got myself good this time," he says, turning his neck back and forth, assessing the damage.

"Does it happen a lot?" I ask, as I go into the cubicle to get some toilet paper for him. He wets it under the cold tap before wiping it over his grazed skin.

"It used to happen a lot more. Not so frequent these days," he says.

"Do you wanna talk about it?" I ask.

He lets out a sigh, throwing the now bloody toilet paper into the trash, eyes dropping to the sink as his hands clutch the bench.

"I don't remember the night Tamsyn found me in the water out by the dock but it's as if my subconscious remembers, you know? The night-mares are always the same. It can be different events that lead to it but in the end, I'm always struggling to breathe, like there's no air. When I wake up it's like I've tried to scratch holes in my throat to get air in," he tells me.

"Have you talked to your therapist about them?" I ask, not sure what to say.

"Yeah, we've worked out a system which works the majority of the time. But since I'm not at home in my own bed, I'm a bit thrown off I think."

"That makes sense. It's different sleeping in a strange bed," I tell him, finding I've had less sleep this week than normal. "You doing okay in general though?" I ask, wanting to make sure his mental health is improving.

He finally lifts his eyes, turning to lean his back against the bench to face me.

"Yeah man, I'm a lot better now. The medication I'm on now is working. I gotta work at keeping my mind in check every day but I'm getting there," he tells me, with a slight smile upon his face.

"That's awesome man. Remember if anything ever happens and you aren't coping, make sure you reach out to someone. I'm always here too," I tell him, looking him dead in the eye, getting my message across.

"I hear ya dude and I will. I promise," he says. "Here let's hug it out then go sneak into Tamsyn's room for you," he says, opening his arms. I close the gap giving him a couple manly taps on his back then break apart. "Lets go," he says and I see a glimpse of the trouble maker Rafe is famous for being.

"You're serious?" I ask, following him as he leads the way, checking for teachers this time.

"Yeah, why not? It's Friday and we are heading home today so not much they will do I reckon. Plus I can be your lookout," he tells me, as I follow him away from our cabins and down the dusty path to where the girls are located. It's still dark out and neither of us know the time but the sun must be sure to make an appearance soon. There's no one out patrolling but we keep to the side where the bushes are, in case we have to hide.

"Do you know which cabin is theirs?" I ask, because I haven't got the slightest idea.

"Yeah, JP and I went with Penny to her cabin before we went to the flying fox the other afternoon."

As the cabins come into view, we slow our steps in case anyone is still keeping an eye out at this time of the night. We creep around by their bathroom but it looks deserted, so I follow Rafe to a cabin near the end. He slowly turns the handle being as quiet as can be, holding his finger to his lips. I step in after him and we each check the beds. I see Penny asleep on the bottom bunk so I know we must be in the right room. My heart beat increases as I climb up and see my girl with her long brown hair fanned out around her.

"Over here," I whisper to Rafe, and he steps over, peeking up at her.

"Cover her mouth," he whispers, with a glint in his eyes. I know he's up to no good but I don't want her to blow our cover, so I cover her mouth as Rafe starts tickling her. Her eyes flash open, widening as she squirms in shock. Her muffled screams try to fill the air, but once she sees it's me she quietens down. I nudge Rafe to stop because he's still tormenting her. I release her mouth and her laboured breaths fill the air. Sitting up, she reaches back, grabs her pillow and whacks Rafe over the head with it, causing him to laugh.

"So not funny," Tamsyn tells him, crossing her arms over her chest.

"Hey why aren't you whacking Tate?" he queries.

"Because that had your name written all over it," she says, angrily. I cup her cheek and her body relaxes as she looks at me. "Hi," she softly says.

"Hi," I reply. "Move over, let me in." She shuffles over so I can climb in, pulling most of her body on top of me so we can both fit in the single bed. Camp beds are definitely designed to prevent anyone getting some action.

"I'll sneak back," Rafe says, about to walk towards the door but Chloe's voice stops him.

"You might get caught and then Tate's cover will be blown," she says.

"True. Anyone got a spare pillow? I'll crash on the floor," Rafe says.

"I wouldn't mind a cuddle if you feel up to being a big spoon?" Chloe surprisingly says, and I lift my head to watch the two of them.

"Sure, I'm always up for cuddles," Rafe cheerily says, turning to me and winking. Chloe squeezes right in next to the wall, and Rafe climbs in behind her. Her audible sigh fills the air.

"Rafe must be a good cuddler," Tamsyn whispers into my ear, which sparks a smile on my face. I press a lingering kiss to her lips, but don't take it any further as we have company. We both settle into the bed, Tamsyn running circles over my ribs where the tattoo of Quinn is. It's something she started doing after I got the tattoo and I'm not even sure she's aware of it but it relaxes us both, always sending us to sleep.

I get woken up by Penny pushing both me and Tamsyn. I squint my eyes open as Tamsyn stretches out her arms, still cradled into my side.

"You better try to sneak back to your cabins because it's light out," Penny tells me, and my ears register Rafe's snores coming from the opposite bunk.

"I'll see you at breakfast," I tell Tamsyn, kissing her lips and climbing down. I start shaking Rafe's back to wake him.

"Aww I don't wanna go, it's comfy here," he says, and I see him squeezing Chloe's body in tighter to his.

"Come on man, I don't wanna get caught," I plead, not wanting to get in trouble on the last day.

"Fine, I'm coming," he relents, releasing Chloe. "Thanks for the snuggles Chlo," he says, and I watch as he kisses the top of her head. She turns in his arms and a strange look passes over both of their faces.

"Right back at ya," she says softly, rolling over as he gets up. I give Tamsyn a final kiss before Rafe and I check the coast is clear then make a mad dash back to our cabin with huge smiles on our faces. We head straight to the bathroom and then casually walk out of them as Mr. Finnegan rounds the corner like we had just gotten up to use the bathroom.

"Morning gentleman," he says, as we pass by him, heading to our cabin. A few others are opening their doors, waking up so it looks like we made it back at the perfect time. Once we get inside the cabin, Rafe holds up his hand with a massive smile on his face. I give him a high five feeling like we accomplished something great.

"Where the hell were you two?" JP barks at us, breaking our moment.

"Snuck in to see the girls in their cabin," I tell him, lowering my voice.

"Why didn't you tell me?" JP whines.

"Sorry cuz, it was a last minute thing," I tell him, knowing he would have wanted to see Penny. It must be the huge smile he sees on Rafe's face that drains the fight out of him because he directs his attention to him.

"Why are you smiling like you had the best night of your life?" he asks him, and I look to Rafe and notice he's sporting the biggest smile I've seen on him in a while. Interesting.

"Just had a good sleep was all," he beams at JP, causing JP's eyes to widen.

"You better not have been in Penny's bed?" JP says, between gritted teeth which makes Rafe laugh. His laughter angers JP more and they start play fighting like little kids.

"I don't kiss and tell," Rafe taunts, causing me to laugh as I know he's just trying to get a rise out of JP and it's working. They keep wrestling until Rafe lies down on the floor laughing. JP can't resist his best friend's laughter and joins in with him.

When we greet the girls at breakfast I say to Tamsyn, "So how did you sleep?" her knowing smile shines my way.

"It was blissful actually," she says, reaching forward to peck my lips.

"I wish camp was longer," Scott says, from the other side of Tamsyn.

"I know, it's been such a great week," Penny says, and we all agree.

"How did you sleep?" I hear JP ask Penny.

"Fine. Why?" she asks him, which has Rafe's shoulders jerking, as he laughs into his bowl of cereal.

"Just asking," JP says casually, catching on to the fact Rafe is messing with him.

"Did you have a good sleep Rafe?" Tamsyn chimes in, knowing where Rafe spent the night.

"It was great," he says, smiling wide at her and winking, infuriating JP more as he isn't in the know.

"Please, someone just tell JP where Rafe slept before he blows a gasket," Scott says, trying to stop himself from laughing at JP's reddening face.

"Oh he was in Chloe's bed," Penny says, which has JP's eyes widening along with Scott's.

"What?" JP says, astonished.

"She gives good cuddles," Rafe tells JP, shrugging his shoulders.

"Man, you guys gossip like girls," Tamsyn teases them, which has everyone laughing and dropping the subject. My observant eyes notice when Chloe and Leyla enter the dining hall, Rafe and Chloe's eyes briefly flick to each other then away again, before they are caught. I don't get a chance to think any more of it because the subject changes to tonight's plans.

"I know camp's finished but do you guys want to have a sleepover at mine tonight?" Tamsyn asks.

"I'm in," I tell her, jumping at the chance to spend time with her.

"Me too," Scott, JP and Penny say, in unison.

"I've got a therapy session but I'll be over after that," Rafe tells us, and now we have plans for a sleepover, it makes the end of camp easier to bear.

That night when I'm cuddled up next to Tamsyn in her bed, I feel like this is the best week I've had in a long time and I hope they continue to be this good. We all deserve some goodness in our lives after the recent tragic events.

Chapter 21

-- Tamsyn --

It's weeks later and camp is all anyone is still talking about. The high felt at camp has followed us home and everyone is still buzzing with the thrill from all the adrenaline filled activities. I tried to keep up with the energy but it's too hard with this pit digging a hole in my stomach. My dad's anniversary is in a few days. A whole year without him. Three hundred and sixty five days of my life he wasn't a part of.

I haven't mentioned it to anyone because I'd rather not think about it. I've withdrawn into myself the last few days and I know it's happening but I can't pull myself out. It's this feeling of wading in water, my legs are working hard under the surface unseen to keep my head above the surface but every now and then, I have to take a big gulp of air because I fear I will sink. My feet never stop and they keep up their furious paddling and I manage to carry on as I am. My body is present but my mind is elsewhere and unable to function as usual.

I've missed conversations because I've been zoned out thinking about my dad and thinking about not thinking about him, which is a vicious cycle. It's turned into a game. If I can hold back my tears a bit longer then maybe it will all fade away. As I sit here while Tate and the others talk, my eyes burn from holding my tears in. They'll float to the edge of my eyelids, ready to fall but at the last second, I draw them back in. I didn't even think it was possible to contain tears like that, but sadly it is. It's easy to hide pain when you don't want anyone to see.

My hair is in a plait today hanging over my shoulder, and while my other hand rests on our lunch table, my fingers twist the end of the plait aimlessly between my fingers. My eyes daydream as they stare at the wooden bench. Breathe, just breathe I tell myself as the tears burn on their way forward again. A firm squeeze on my thigh jerks me out of my daydream and before I can pull the tears back from sight, my eyes glance up to who squeezed my leg. Tate.

Anguish crosses his face as he must catch the glassiness I know will be shining in my eyes. While the others continue talking, unaware, Tate leans forward pressing his lips to my forehead. His gentle gesture makes the tears finally release down my cheeks. He lifts his leg over the bench seat then without warning, he bends down and gathers me in his arms. My legs cinch his waist and as my arms snake around his neck, I bury my face by his throat and let all the pain out. He squeezes me tighter as he walks away.

"Tate?" I hear Rafe call, causing him to turn around. I feel his throat move as if he's shaking his head then he's on the move again. My hot tears burn tracks running down my cheeks as they find their destination, soaking his shirt. Vaguely I hear a door close and then other doors banging around. My butt and thighs get seated on a cool surface as Tate runs his arms down my back. My body clings to him so tightly.

"Baby, please you're scaring me. What is it?" he pleads, and it just makes me cry harder, wishing my dad was here. He wraps his arms back around me, cupping my head and holding it into his neck. As if he's telling me to let it all out for him to absorb through his skin. So that's what I do. I cry until my throat is raw and the whole time Tate's grip on me doesn't loosen.

When I'm empty from all my tears and emotions, I break contact with his neck and he feels the movement, letting me look up into his eyes. His own tears shimmer in his eyes as he stares at the devastation on my face. Gently he wipes under my eyes with his thumbs, removing the remnants of my pain.

"Talk to me," he softly says, staring into my grief filled eyes. I take an audible breath which makes me shiver.

"It's Dad's anniversary on Thursday," I tell him, feeling some remaining tears leak down with my words. I see the moment his face cracks. Feeling my pain. This is what connects us. Our grief has always pulled our souls together. What one feels, the other feels because of what we've gone through. So he knows exactly how I'm feeling right now. A single tear drops from his cheek and I swipe it away. He leans forward and rests his forehead on mine. Our pain surrounds us, filling the air as we breathe each other in, lost in our thoughts. His arms loosely surround me.

"Will this ever get any easier?" I ask him, not knowing how I can continue to carry on feeling this pain for the rest of my life.

"I sure hope so, Sweetness," he says, knowing he feels the same. The bell for class goes but neither of us moves. I feel his hand moving before he's talking into his phone.

"Hey man," then a pause, "Yeah she's okay. Did someone grab our bags?" then he looks into my eyes. "Thanks man, I think we are just gonna walk back to her house now," he says into the phone, but I know he's asking me, so I nod. "Nah man, we'll be fine. Just ring me when you're there after school. Thanks man," he says, before hanging up and pocketing his phone. "JP has our bags, he'll bring them by your place after school," he informs me. All I can do is nod. If I talk, the tears will unleash again. "You ready to wag school with me Sweetness?" he asks, his lip lifting on one side and I can't help but offer him a small smile of my own.

He pulls me down so my feet land on the cold tiled floor then he draws me into his chest. The thumping of his heart helps to calm my wild thoughts. Everyone will be in class now but we wait a few more minutes before exiting. It's the bathroom he took me to before, around the side of the gym. Holding hands, we walk quickly down the side of classrooms, headed to the back gate of the school. The front gate is right by the office so it's more likely we will get seen that way. Neither of us care about the consequences of wagging, we just want to escape.

As soon as the iron gate comes into view, we take off into a sprint, running straight through it and down the street before we slow to catch our breaths.

"Hop on my back, Sweetness," Tate suggests, bending down in front of me. I wrap my arms around his neck as he grabs my thighs and wraps my legs around him. I jiggle on his back as he walks, breathing in his earthy scent to calm me down some more. I don't know what would have become of me without him to pull me out of my head. He's saved me in more ways than he realises.

-- Tate --

When I reach her front porch, I lower her to her feet. We had to take the long way back to her house since we came out the back gate of school, but it didn't bother me. Any time I get to spend with her is a blessing. She walks over to one of the potted plants on the far side of the porch and pushes it on an angle to grab the spare key, hidden under there. Unlocking the door, we step inside and head up to her room.

Her mum is still at work so it's just the two of us. Entering her room I pull her into my arms, needing to hold her close. The despair on her face at school broke me. I hate seeing her so upset. Her dad's anniversary. I didn't even think it might be coming up soon. She's been much happier lately but as we both know, it only takes one little thing to knock you off track, where your pain tumbles out and pushes you down again.

178

She pulls her head away, bending her neck back to look up at me.

"You okay?" I ask, as I watch the sadness flicker in her eyes.

She leans forward taking my lips in hers before she softly says against them, "Make me forget, please?" I pull back to look in her eyes and her visible pain cuts me open. "Please?" she pleads, knowing that I want to tell her no.

I search her eyes before asking, "You sure?" and she nods. If I can take away her pain for a minute, I can't deny her. I grab her neck pulling her to me, kissing her with all the love I have inside. I lift her in my arms, walking us back to the bed. We both start ripping the other's clothes off, and in seconds we're naked. Our pants fill the silent air. She grabs a condom from her bedside table and rips it open before sliding it on me.

As I line up with her entrance, I kiss her deeply before entering her all the way. I swallow down her gasps as I start to move. Rocking my hips back and forth, I lean up on my hands and stare into her eyes.

"I love you," I mouth, and as a tear slips down her cheek, I lean forward and lick it's trail before kissing her nose.

"I love you too," she mouths back, and I speed up my movements. My thumb rubs against her little bundle of nerves and I watch her face, as I feel her tighten around me. Her moans fill the air as our sweat slicked bodies move against each other. "Tate," she groans out, as I feel the pull of her. Her hips lift off the bed as she's taken over the edge. A few more thrusts and then I'm following her with my own release, my body covering her as I groan into her throat.

"You okay?" I ask her, as I look into her eyes.

"I'm good. I promise," she says, lifting up and kissing me. As I slide out of her, I pull her into my chest and we lie there, relishing being in each other's arms. After about ten minutes, I suggest we take a shower before her mum comes home. Quickly showering together, I then get changed back into my uniform and she changes into her usual tank top and sleep shorts.

Just as she returns from taking our towels to the bathroom, the front door slams and grabs our attention.

"Tamsyn?" we hear her mum's worried voice ring through the house. We rush out of the bedroom door and are greeted by her mum, running up the stairs. "Oh thank God, you're here. The school rang and I was worried as I couldn't reach you on your phone," she says, clutching her chest.

"Sorry Mum, I didn't mean to worry you," Tamsyn says, cringing.

"Is everything okay?" she asks, looking between us, her eyes settling on Tamsyn. All it does is set Tamsyn off again. She rushes to her Mum's arms, her tears returning. All the pain she released back at school, is released all over again.

Her mum clutches her in her arms saying, "Shh, it's okay bub. It's okay." She looks at me, questioning me about what's happened without saying a word.

I softly say, "Vince's anniversary," which has her mum's breath hitching, and her own tears falling.

"Just let it all out," Tanya tells Tamsyn, as they stand there gripping tightly onto each other. My phone ringing has me reaching into my pocket quickly, not wanting to disturb them. I answer since it's JP.

"You here man?" I ask him.

"Yeah, I'm outside. You coming?" he asks.

"Yeah, be there in a minute," I say, before hanging up. "Sweetness, JP is here now. Will you be okay if I leave?" I ask, as her sobs quieten. She moves her head so I can see her bloodshot eyes.

"Do you think you'll be allowed to stay the night?" my broken girl asks. I look to Tanya for permission and she nods, not wanting to deny her daughter when she's in this state.

"I'll ask when I get home. I'm not sure if I'll be in trouble for cutting class," I tell her truthfully, knowing my aunt and uncle will probably be gearing up to tell me off.

"Okay, let me know please?" she says.

"I will," I say, leaning forward and kissing the top of her head and then leaning across, I kiss the top of Tanya's head too, knowing they could both use the comfort. "Bye," I say as I walk down the stairs to meet JP so I can go home to face the consequences.

"It's her dad's anniversary in a few days," I tell JP, as soon as I get in the car, knowing it would be his first question.

"Oh shit, she okay?" he asks, worry leaking into his voice as he drives us home.

"She's a wreck man. Her mum just got home. She wants me to come back tonight but I'll see if your parents will let me," I tell him.

"They'll understand once you explain it to them," JP says.

His mum is waiting for us once we get inside, arms crossed, her foot tapping on the floor. I spew the explanation at her before she can even start yelling at me for ditching school and her features soften. Her arms unfold.

"Aww poor girl, is she okay?" she asks.

"She's with her mum now but they wondered if I could go back and stay the night please?" I ask, hoping. She stares at me for a good minute before answering.

"Fine but only because I'm worried about Tamsyn. And no more skipping school or I will tell your parents next time," she tells me.

"Thanks aunty Sharon," I say, leaning forward and kissing her cheek. I hurry to my room and get changed. I quickly get my homework done too since I feel guilty about missing the afternoon classes. I knock on JP's door later and ask if he can drop me off at Tamsyn's.

When we pull up to the curb I grab both our bags, mine full with my packed uniform for tomorrow. Tamsyn's swollen eyes greet me as I knock on the door and I draw her straight into my side. We walk up the stairs to her room and hop under the bed covers and settle in to watch the movie she was playing before I arrived. She snuggles into my side, her cheek resting on my chest and that's how we remain for another movie. In silence, I hold her tight, letting her be with her thoughts. Letting her grieve for her dad all over again.

Chapter 22
~

-- Tamsyn --

It's been a few weeks since my dad's anniversary and I'm back to feeling lighter. It's amazing what one day can make you feel. Mum and I both stayed home and openly grieved for Dad on his anniversary. We went down to his grave which we both hadn't been able to face since his funeral. We left some flowers there for him because his grave looked bare, which made me sad and I promised myself I would try to visit him more often now.

Tate came and stayed the night after school too and held me while I cried. Comforting me the best way he could. When I woke in the morning, it was weird. It was like everything had reverted back to normal. There were no more tears or sad feelings churning around. Like a weight had been lifted. Dad's first anniversary was so heavy. I wonder if all his birthdays and anniversaries will feel the same or if they will get better in time.

Since then Penny, the guys and I have knuckled down and put more work into studying. Our usual sleepovers have become regular study sessions and it's making us think seriously about the future and what we want to do with our lives. We are now on our two week holiday break before we go back for the last term of the year. We've been getting together nearly every day, revising and working on assignments. Scott has turned into a studying general, keeping us in line.

But today we are having a night off as it's Penny's eighteenth birthday. She's throwing a big bash at her place. Most of the school are planning to attend. They always go nuts when they hear there's a party at hers and this occasion is no exception.

I bought her a new dress to wear as her present so I asked Tate to drive with me over there a few hours early, so I can give it to her. The guys and I are crashing at her place afterwards so Tate will drive my car home for us the next day. My driving has improved and my mum has taken me for some lessons as well but I still need to work on my confidence. Instructor Tate is treating today as another lesson which will be the furthest I've driven so far.

We manage to arrive at Penny's without any hiccups and Tate's proud smile beams at me as we pull up to her place.

"You're getting better, Sweetness," he tells me.

"Thanks, I feel like I'm improving," I reply.

"I'm sure you'll be ready to sit your test soon, the way you are going."

"Thanks," I reply, leaning across the car to give him a kiss.

He grabs my carefully wrapped box from the back seat along with his smaller wrapped present. Knocking on Penny's door, she opens it letting us in.

"Happy Birthday," Tate and I shout, which has Penny laughing at us.

"Hey guys, thanks, come in," she says. "Follow me, I'll show you guys to your room down here, if you wanna dump your stuff. If everyone wants to crash together, we can always pull the mattresses out later or something."

"Cool, sounds like a plan," Tate says, following behind me. Entering the room, we place our bags on the bed and then turn to Penny. "These are from us," Tate says, handing over the presents.

"Aww, thanks so much guys. Can I open them now?" she asks, with a twinkle in her eye.

"Go ahead," I tell her, which is the only motivation she needs before ripping into the paper of my present. When she pulls the A-line, off the shoulder, short baby pink skater dress out of the box, her eyes widen, admiring it.

"Oh my gosh, it's gorgeous guys," she says, her eyes dancing with excitement.

"That's why we had to come over early so you can wear it tonight," I tell her. Her huge smile shines at us. "Open the other one."

She places the dress carefully on the bed before ripping the wrapping on Tate's smaller package. She pulls out the matching headband we got with pale pink flowers adorning it and some new silver hoop earrings.

"Aww guys, honestly these are amazing. Thank you," she says, wrapping us both up in a big hug. "I can't wait to get ready now," she says, clear excitement leaking out of her.

"Do you need help with any setting up?" Tate asks.

"Nah, I'm not doing anything I don't usually do. You can help move some of the bottles to the table, but apart from that we are good to go," she says.

"Well actually, JP sent me with supplies and I have strict instructions," Tate says, smiling at us. He reaches into his bag, pulling out bags of balloons and a huge gold banner that says, 'Happy Birthday,' across it.

"Well we better start blowing these up then," I say, and we all rip open a packet of balloons and get started.

An hour and a half later, we have so many balloons blown up they take up all the floor space in the living room. It actually looks quite cool, like a moshpit of balloons. Tate and I managed to hang the birthday banner in there too so when people come through the front door, it'll be the first thing they see.

"I'm gonna go shower and get ready guys," Penny tells us. She walks down to her room and a few minutes later, we hear the shower starting. Tate wastes no time, his cheeky grin directed at me as he picks me up under my legs and starts kicking balloons out of the way. I giggle as they go flying around us before he drops to the floor, lowering me to the carpet, surrounded by all the different colours. He kisses me with a hunger we both feel these days whenever we are around each other. His body lowers over me and I wrap my legs around his waist, getting lost in the moment. I can feel the latex of the balloons lightly against my whole body as they shift with our movements. The loud bang of one balloon popping pulls us from the moment, our heated gazes look at each other.

"Damn, I can't get enough of you," he softly says, giving me a light kiss to my lips before helping me up. We step around the balloons, careful not to pop anymore and then sit on the couch just in time for Penny to come out in her dress.

"Aww you look beautiful," I tell her, which has her gushing.

"Thanks. I love this dress. I think it's my new favourite," she says, twirling around letting the hem swing around her. "Come on you two, go get ready, people will start showing up soon," she says, pulling me from the seat and pushing me towards the room.

-- Tate --

Chapter 22

JP, Scott and Rafe arrived after I finished changing, while the girls disappeared into Penny's room to do their hair and makeup. We make us some drinks while we wait and then head out to the pool to drink them. The sun is just about to set so it's still early. Most people won't show up until it's dark out.

When Penny and Tamsyn walk out to the pool area, Tamsyn steals my breath away. She's wearing a simple black halter knee length dress. Her long hair is curled behind her and her eyes are darkened with makeup which makes the blue of her eyes even brighter. I don't even realise my feet have taken me to her until I'm leaning down kissing her, not caring about the others and the fact they are probably looking at us.

We pull apart breathless and she says, "You couldn't wait for me to walk over to you?" with a hint of a smile in her voice.

"My feet led me to you of their own accord. They'll always lead me to you because they know where I belong," I tell her, truthfully. This girl has captured my heart and I don't ever want it back if it means I get to have her. I watch as her cheeks darken from my words.

"Get a room you two," Rafe teases behind us, and Tamsyn's cheeks darken even more as I turn us around, pulling her back into my front, encasing her in my arms. The others laugh as I smile at them with happiness only Tamsyn can ignite in me.

We move back into the house as people start to arrive and the music gets turned up louder. Tamsyn and Penny head through the crowd to the kitchen to make themselves drinks, so I follow. Their laughter fills the air and I catch sight of JP standing off to the side, watching Penny as he drinks from his plastic cup.

"What are you doing over here looking at her like a creeper?" I ask, taking a sip from my own cup.

His grin is directed my way but his eyes stay on Penny as he says, "Just making sure she's safe without interfering in the fun."

"Gotcha," I reply, taking a wide stance next to him, fixing my gaze on Tamsyn. We both keep an eye on our girls while they laugh and sip from their cups, their buzz taking hold the longer the night goes on. "Where are Scott and Rafe?" I ask.

"I think they're out by the fire pit, talking to Elijah and Tyler," he tells me, his focus still on Penny. As the song changes, the girls suddenly stop and then together, start jumping around at the excitement the song brings. Penny grabs Tamsyn's hand while they carry their drinks and head into the throng of people, dancing and kicking up the balloons we'd blown up earlier. Several have popped but there's still enough covering the floor so it can't be seen properly. We watch the girls get lost in the crowd and it isn't until the song changes that JP nudges me.

"Come on that's long enough, let's go find them," he says, which has me laughing as I skull my drink, leaving the cup on the bench.

"You've got it bad man," I tell him, and he just grunts at me which makes me laugh harder as I follow after him. When the girls come into view in the middle of the swaying bodies, both JP and I move instinc-tively behind our girls. I hear Tamsyn's intake of breath.

"It's me, Sweetness," I whisper in her ear, causing her body to relax into me. She pushes herself back into my chest and we dance to the music. I intertwine our fingers and put my arm across her chest, pulling her closer to me. We lose ourselves in the music, and everything drifts away as I focus on my girl.

Lifting my head from her neck a few songs later, JP gives me a head nod, as he leads Penny off the dance floor. I continue to dance with Tamsyn for another song before yelling in her ear to be heard over the music.

"Lets go," I say, spinning her around in my arms and leading her out the back door.

Chloe passes us on our way saying ,"Hey guys," which has Tamsyn stopping and smiling at her.

"Hey Chloe, you okay? Where's Leyla?" I ask, as she's by herself. And even though we are at Penny's, I don't like the idea of any girls being alone while around so many drunk people.

"She's uh back there. I'm just going to the bathroom. Have a good night guys," she stutters, as she continues walking past us slowly. I continue leading Tamsyn away from the house but it's only a few steps until we are met by Rafe.

"Rafe," Tamsyn squeals in her drunkenness, leaping into Rafe's arms and it makes me realise she must have had more to drink than I realise.

"Hey Petal, you alright?" he asks, his huge smile forming when he realises Tamsyn is drunk. He lowers her to her feet, keeping his hands on her shoulders, steadying her.

"I'm A okay," she says, which has Rafe looking at me with a raised brow and trying not to laugh.

"We're just getting some air," I tell Rafe, and he nods. "Where you going?"

"Back inside to see what's going on in there," he says. "Look after her," he tells me.

"You know it," I tell him, bumping his fist. I pull Tamsyn to carry on our way and she stumbles which has my gaze shifting to her. In my peripheral something catches my eye and I first see Chloe then Rafe close behind, both walking around the side of the house. Neither of them entered and went where they said they were.

I was going to take Tamsyn to the fire pit but change my mind and divert to the pool instead. The last wooden pool chair where she found me so many months ago is empty so I walk us down there and pull her down next to me as I lie down. She shifts her head so she can look above us at the stars.

"There aren't as many here as there was at camp," she says, and I agree. We're both quiet for a minute before she breaks it saying, "Do you think it's possible for us to always be together?" and her words make my heart beat faster.

"Why are you asking that?" I say quietly, squeezing her into my side.

"Did you know only like two percent of high school relationships last?" she asks, and it makes me chuckle.

"Sweetness, did you google that?" and her scrunched up face has me laughing louder as she says, "Maybe," which only makes me laugh more. I pull her on top of me so I can look into her eyes.

Searching her gaze, I see the vulnerability in them and I let out a sigh before saying, "I don't know what the future holds Sweetness and both of us know how short life can be. But I don't think I have a say in the matter. You've already stolen my heart completely and if for some reason we go our separate ways, I can promise my feet will always lead me back to you." Her glassy eyes stare at me and as she blinks, the first tears drop down. I pull her head to my chest, holding onto her as tightly as possible, hoping we never have to be without the other.

"We'll always have the stars," she barely whispers.

"We'll always have the stars," I agree.

In the early hours of the morning when everyone is gone, I find JP in the living room throwing a blanket over Scott on the couch as I carry a sleeping Tamsyn in my arms.

"Penny's asleep in her room, so I'll just crash in there with her," he says.

"Sweet, Tamsyn and I will just crash in the other room," I tell him, about to turn around and walk down the hall but the front door opens, and Rafe walks through.

"Where have you been?" JP asks his best friend, who casually shrugs his shoulders.

"There were a couple of girls lingering around. I just walked them to their car to be safe," he says, with the smallest hint of a smile on his lips. I can't help but think he's been with Chloe this whole time but if he's not going to say anything, neither am I.

JP throws a spare pillow at Rafe who catches it easily, "Tate and I are crashing in the rooms with the girls, you wanna pull a mattress in there or you wanna crash out here with Scott?" he asks.

"I'll crash on the couch with Scotty, you guys go to your girls," he says, as he turns to lie down on the other couch, kicking his shoes off.

"You good, bro?" JP asks him.

Lifting his eyes to JP he says, "Yeah dude, I am. Promise," he says. And that one word makes JP visibly relax like they have a rule between them. That if Rafe says promise, he's telling the truth. I understand how JP must feel, always worried about his best friend, never knowing exactly what is going on in his head.

"Night," we all say, as JP and I walk down the hall to the bedrooms. I lay Tamsyn on the bed while I pull back the covers and then shuffle her under. Lifting her dress, I pull it off her sleeping form and strip down to my boxers and then slide in behind her. Holding her tightly to me, her words from earlier swim in my head. Do you think we'll always be together? My heart gallops at the very thought we might not be together in the future but I know with certainty, there was a truth in my own words. If something does happen, my feet will always lead me back to her.

Don't Fade. Breathe Easy.

Chapter 23

-- Tamsyn --

The closer we get to the end of the school year, the faster time goes. It's as if it's slipping through my fingers and I can't slow it down, no matter how hard I try. There's just this feeling hanging over my head that Tate and I are coming to an end and I can't shake it.

It's already a few weeks into the last term of school and our school ball is this Saturday night. Mum has booked me in to get my hair and makeup done as well as manicures and pedicures for the both of us. We went and bought a dress in the school holidays and I can't wait for Tate to see me in it. It's a dark green mermaid satin dress with a dipping v neck and a long split up the side.

On the Saturday morning of our school ball, Mum and I go to the nail salon and get our nails done first. The guys organised for a limo to take us so we are all meeting at my place with their parents for them to get photos of us before we go.

After our nails, we have lunch and then Mum takes me to get my hair and makeup done. I get loose curls put in and a natural makeup with brown tones which makes my blue eyes pop. When we get home I have a quick shower all the while managing not to mess up my hair or makeup. As I slip on the satin material, I call in Mum to tie it up. Once she sees me, she loses it and tears shine in her eyes.

"Aww bub you look absolutely gorgeous," she gushes, pulling me into a hug. She pulls the straps at the back, tying them tightly and then hands me some of her dangling earrings to wear. I have to sit down to get my small black heels strapped on. I've only just finished buckling the second shoe when we hear knocking on the front door, so Mum rushes down the stairs to open it.

The commotion from downstairs sounds like everyone has arrived so I take a deep breath and walk out the door. Nobody notices my entrance until I start coming down the stairs and all the talking stops, everyone's eyes are on me. I can feel my cheeks heat under their gazes but my eyes only focus on Tate. He looks extremely handsome in his three piece black suit.

As I make it to the bottom of the stairs, he's shaken out of his haze and takes the few steps to me, kissing my cheek.

"You look breathtaking, Sweetness," he whispers, so only I can hear and I know my face color is deepening.

"You scrub up pretty good yourself," I tell him, which makes his smile grow.

"I got you this," he says, holding out a plastic container with a corsage in it. He opens it, takes it out and slides it onto my wrist.

"It's beautiful," I tell him, looking at the delicate purple flowers with the sprinkled white spots. "It looks like."

"The stars?" he finishes for me, and I nod, holding his gaze. "That's because these flowers are called night sky petunias. They look like they have the galaxy painted on them." We stare at each other and I can't

194

believe this perfect boy is mine. "I'd give you the real thing if I could, Sweetness," he whispers in my ear, before delivering a soft kiss to my cheek. "I know it doesn't match your dress," he says, but I stop him.

"It's perfect and I love it," I confess. Holding my hand to my chest, I finally break his gaze and take everyone else in. Rafe, Scott and JP are all wearing different coloured suits. Rafe is in a light grey, JP is in a navy blue and Scott is in a charcoal grey.

"Wow, look at you guys. You guys look great," I tell them, and everyone is all smiles. All their parents are here too. Only Tate's are missing but he's promised to send lots of photos. Another knock on the door has my mum answering it and in walks Penny, followed by her parents. She looks stunning in a light purple tulle dress that flows to the ground. Her hair is curled but piled strategically on her head in an updo. Her eyes automatically find JP and I glance to him to see the huge smile he has at seeing her.

"You look amazing Penny," I say, pulling her into my arms.

"You look beautiful Tam," she replies, her eyes scanning my dress with appreciation.

"Okay, let's get some photos first, shall we?" my mum says, and everyone stands next to each other with arms around the person next to them. We then get some individual ones and Tate and I and Penny and JP take some couple photos. Rafe and Scott even take a photo together since they are going stag tonight.

"I've got some bottles of wine for the parents if you'd like some?" Mum says, leading all the parents to the kitchen. It's nice to know Mum has made friends with the guy's parents as well. Me and the others take some selfies on our phones while the parents are occupied.

"Limo should be here in a minute if you need to grab anything?" Scott says, so I grab my matching clutch from upstairs and then we say goodbye to our parents. The limo ride to the Brookwater Function Centre at the golf course is filled with all of us laughing and chatting about what to expect once we get there.

It's supposed to be a casino royale theme so they have the round tables decorated as poker and blackjack tables. None of us dressed up in themed attire but when we see others, there are a few who clearly have tried to follow the theme. Everyone mills around the entrance, taking more selfies before entering. Tate holds my hand the whole way through to our seats.

We manage to find a table where we can all sit together and Chloe and Leyla even join us. Since camp I've let go of the anger I've held towards them about the Blake situation and I can see the girls I had initially become friends with, all those years ago. Our friendship will probably never go back to the way it was but I'm happy to see where it goes from here on out. They look gorgeous in their gowns. Leyla in red and Chloe in gold.

Over the microphone, Mr. Barnes tells everyone to take a seat so they can get started with dinner. It's a buffet so every table takes turns going up and selecting their food. Once dinner is over, the dancing will commence. The charged atmosphere surrounds us as everyone is having a good time.

The teachers are acting as chaperones for the night and watching everyone with hawk eyes. Mr. Finnegan has his eyes glued to the punch bowl making sure it doesn't get spiked with alcohol.

As soon as the music starts, everyone is on their feet and moving to the dance floor. The songs fade into each other as I sway with Tate while the others surround us. Smiles light up all our faces. Soon sweat is dripping down my back from the dancing but I don't let it bother me, as I don't want to miss a minute of the excitement.

I gaze around the dance floor and notice Chloe facing Rafe with her arms around his neck and he's holding her tight to him, whispering in her ear. An authentic smile shines from his face which makes my heart feel lighter at seeing him happy. He looks up at that moment and catches my eye, giving me a wink.

The next song to play is 'Wild Things' by Alessia Cara. It's the song that sent Tate into a panic in JP's car so I still my movements as soon as I realise. Tate spins me around so I'm facing him and moves my hands up to wrap around his neck, while his hands slip to my lower back, pulling me close.

"It's okay, Sweetness. I've got control over it. It's not gonna trigger me this time," he tells me, but I'm still unsure. I know he hasn't been triggered in a while but it still lingers in the back of my mind that anything could. With his hand, he runs his index finger down my cheek softly. "Come on, where's that smile I love?" he says, his eyes following the route his finger takes. As his finger runs over my chin, down my neck and across my collarbone I can't help but laugh as he hits a ticklish part. "There it is," he says, his own smile matching mine. Leaning forward, his mouth coaxes my lips open and we lose ourselves while the song that once triggered him, plays in the background.

After a few more songs, the music gets stopped briefly as they announce king and queen of the ball. Our group screams with excitement as Rafe and Penny get called up. I glance to JP to see his reaction while I continue my cheering. He surprisingly wears a big smile on his face, cheering and clapping along with everyone else.

Once Rafe reaches the stage and his crown gets placed on his head, the huge smile he is known for spreads across his face. He takes Penny's hand as she gets crowned and then he bows while she curtseys, making everyone laugh.

Making their way to the dance floor, the crowd parts and forms a circle around them so they can have their slow dance as king and queen. Half way through the song, Rafe leads Penny over to JP, hands her over to him and bows again. I don't think he realises people bow to the king, not the other way around. JP shakes his head, smiling at his best friend and pats him on the shoulder before he takes over the dance with Penny. Everyone else partners up and fills the dance floor once again.

As the night comes to a close we all gather in the limo and get driven to Penny's where we are having the after party. I gave Penny some clothes for me to take to hers earlier in the week so I could change out of my dress. I slip into my skinny jeans and tank top as soon as we get there, before everyone else starts arriving. Her parents have made themselves scarce again which they usually do. Tate removes his jacket and rolls up the sleeves of his white shirt and my heartbeat picks up. He looks even better like this.

He gives me a knowing smile when he sees my gaze on him and whispers in my ear, "Don't drink too much, I want to have some fun with you later," and my cheeks must look like bright strawberries from my blush.

As always Penny's place gets filled with people. Since it's the usual place for parties I think everyone just assumed it would be the place for the after party. The buzzing atmosphere from earlier has followed us here and everyone drinks and dances until their hearts are content. Rafe and Penny continue to wear their crowns for the rest of the party. Tate and I slip away early into our room and decide to explore each other's bodies for the remainder of the night. I couldn't have asked for a better end to a perfect night.

Chapter 24
~

-- Tate --

Today is the day we start presenting our English assignments on what we are grateful for. Mr. Barnes reckons it will probably take us all week to get through them all. The first few people do theirs and it's much of the same things people are grateful for.

My name gets called third so I take my place at the front of the class, wiping my sweaty palms on my pant legs. I hand the usb drive over to Mr. Barnes for him to set up my slideshow I created.

My mum had to help and send me through photos as I didn't have many with me. It was Quinn's journal that inspired me when I was flicking through it one day. I can only read bits at a time so I still haven't managed to read all she's written but I will get there one day.

Taking a deep breath in and then releasing it I start, "Most of you won't know this but I'm a twin. My twin Quinn and I were born three minutes apart and like most twins we were inseparable. We did everything together." Photos flash across from the whiteboard behind me where the slideshow is projected. The first photos are mainly of the two of us as babies so I talk about that time.

"I would call Quinn, Quinny or flower queen as she loved daisies. And she would call me tater tot which made me feel like I got the short end of the stick when it came to nicknames," my joke has the class laughing. I glance at Tamsyn, her eyes shining with pride at me talking about Quinn because she knows how hard it is.

"You know that saying the calm before the storm? Well Quinn was the calm and the storm. She had moments when she was gentle and quiet but then the next minute, she would be yelling from the top of her lungs about something she was passionate about. Her bedroom was always hit by her storm tendencies too and at times you couldn't even see the floor because so many things covered it. But God forbid you tried to sneak in there and get something without her knowing, because like a sixth sense she would know you had been in there even if you hadn't touched a thing." I take another breath, steadying myself as a picture of her once messy room flashes on the projection.

"As Quinn and I got older, we started to drift apart. It wasn't anything big that started to separate us but just small things like different groups of friends and different interests. I didn't realise at the time that those differences would push us too far from each other." The picture I have of our big front red door flashes up as I continue. "Quinn was quirky and that was one of the things I loved about her. This is the front door of our house which she insisted she wanted painted red. And what Quinn wanted, she got. She had a determination in her that when she set her mind to something there was no changing it, no matter what. She loved bright colours and adrenaline rushes. She was a true lover of life until sadly she didn't love it anymore," I gulp, as I feel my eyes burn. I look to Tamsyn for strength and her own watery eyes stare at me. She offers me a small nod and slight smile, so I breathe and carry on.

"You see, Quinn my twin, my other half, she committed suicide," I state. Gasps fill the air at my words. Only the front row of Scott, Tamsyn and Penny remain unaffected as they already know my story. "When I went back home earlier in the year, it was for her funeral and it was then I came across her journal," I say, as some pictures of things she'd written flash up. I didn't take many, not wanting to share too many of Quinn's thoughts but I took pictures of some of the quotes plus the poem she wrote.

"From the words that Quinn wrote in her journal, I could see how much she was struggling, but in our day to day lives she seemed normal, like everything was fine. I never suspected that she wasn't coping. There was never any sign or if there was, I never noticed. And I will probably live with the guilt of not seeing it for a long time. The guilt of not being able to save her." I blow out a shaky breath coming to the end of my speech.

"So in answer to the question, what am I grateful for? The answer is, I'm grateful for Quinn. I'm grateful I had her as a twin and that I have the good memories we shared which I can hang on to. I'm grateful for her journal because the words she wrote down helped me see I was headed down a dangerous dark path like her. Her words helped me seek help and I know that if I hadn't found her journal, I probably would have sunk further into the darkness. Lastly I'm grateful that I'm alive. Thank you," I say, as the last photo of the display shows the picture of me I took over the weekend. My smiling face in a selfie that I took in my room. I wait as the room erupts in clapping and cheers. I look to Mr. Barnes and he gives me a sad smile as his own hands clap loudly.

He hands me back my usb stick and says, "Well done, Tate," patting me on the back as I move to take my seat next to Tamsyn. Her small hand grabs mine under the table and squeezes it, letting me know with her gesture that she's proud of me.

"That was beautiful, Tate," she whispers, and since my throat feels tight, I rub my thumb back and forth over her hand, instead of using words.

-- Tamsyn --

I'm so proud of Tate. His speech was amazing but I could see how much it pained him to talk about Quinn. He was strong though and powered through it. After class, I ask Mr. Barnes if I can leave my cylinder container with him. It holds my presentation and he said he's happy to place it in his cupboard for me for safe keeping. There were only a couple of people who got to do their speeches today so the rest of us have to wait until later in the week. I'm nervous to do mine but I hope it goes smoothly. I don't have to wait too long because on Wednesday, my name is called.

"Tamsyn, you're up," Mr. Barnes says. Tate gives my thigh a squeeze for encouragement before I stand and walk to Mr. Barnes's desk where he has my hidden collage. I open the container but keep it rolled up so I can talk for a bit. With a shaky exhale, I start my speech.

"When we were first given this assignment, it wasn't hard for me to think of what I was grateful for. Every day we were to write a different thing or something new we were grateful for but my mind would always come back to the first thing I wrote down. It was my first thought and every day it remained the thing I was most grateful for." I look to the front row and Penny, Scott and Tate all watch me intensely, my words keeping their attention. The rest of the room is silent, listening.

"My dad died last year and when he died, he took a part of me with him and I haven't been able to get it back. Every day that went on without him, the bigger that missing part grew until I didn't recognise myself in the mirror anymore. I didn't realise at the time that I was pushing those closest to me away, and even if I did realise what I was doing, I don't know if I could have stopped it. When you lose someone who means so much to you, it breaks your heart so fully that it feels like you will never be the same person you were before you lost them." I take a pause, letting my words sink in. "For a time, my grief was all I knew. To me I didn't think anything I showed to the outside world was different. I pretended I was fine but I was really breaking inside," I say, as a tear leaks down my face.

"It wasn't until someone saw beyond what I showed the world and looked closely at me. They saw the hurt I was hiding and helped me on my journey to heal. I still have a lot of healing to do but you helped me start what I couldn't have done on my own." I lock eyes with Tate and he stares intently at me, waiting. "Sometimes when you reach your lowest point, you need a helping hand to lift you back up," I say. With shaking hands, I uncurl the rolled up collage I made and hold it out, for everyone to see. I hear a sharp intake of breath and I know exactly where it's come from. Tate.

My collage is filled with all the notes he's ever sent me. From the pictures of the stars he drew, the photo of the butterfly, the message he wrote on my thigh in human bio and the rainbow bff. I even redrew the rainbow he drew at our senior retreat. There's also the note where I know he just wanted me to smile. The note where he wrote 'You are enough' is there too, right next to the one where he said his heart belongs to me. I also managed to get a photo of the TNT that he carved into the concrete. I added a photo of my bracelet and necklace he gave me for my birthday and I even gently pulled off a petal from my corsage he gave me and managed to tape it to the collage too. In the very centre of my collage is a big red heart with all his notes surrounding it.

"I'm grateful for the helping hand I received from a boy who didn't know me and who didn't owe me anything. He saw me when the rest of the world didn't and no matter what the future holds, I will forever be grateful for that. I will forever be grateful because your heart saved me, Tate. You saved me," I say, my eyes focused on the boy in front of me who I love. Hoping he can hear my unspoken words. I know guilt eats at him that he couldn't save Quinn but I'm hoping I can ease it a tiny bit by letting him know that he saved me. I can feel the hot tears, run down my face as the emotion overwhelms me. Tate pushes his chair back, comes around the desk and cups my cheeks in his hands.

"You saved me too," he whispers, before capturing my lips with his. The cheering from everyone is deafening as we let our love for each other fill the air.

"Alright, alright, settle down everyone. Well done, Miss Winter, you can take a seat now," Mr. Barnes tells me, and I glance at him where he's smiling at me. Tate holds my hand under the table for the rest of the class.

When the bell signaling the end of the lesson goes, Tate leans close and whispers in my ear, "Thank you, Sweetness," before kissing me lightly on the cheek.

"I meant every word," I tell him, hoping he understands how different my life may have been if he hadn't entered it.

"I'm grateful for you too, you know?" he says.

"I know," I reply, pecking him on the lips before we pack up our things to leave.

After school Tate and I are in my room, sitting on my bed and he has my collage spread out in front of him, looking over all his notes.

"What's with this little smiley face? I don't remember this," he says, pointing to a doodle I'd drawn in one of the corners.

A smile tugs at my lips as I say, "Pass me your human bio book." His brows pull together but he locates the book in his bag and passes it to me. I flick to the back, inside the cover and show him the same little doodle I'd left for him so long ago. Now I know he never noticed the doodle. His eyes widen as he looks at it then glances at me.

"When did you do this?" he asks, shock in his voice from not knowing it was there.

"It was when I borrowed your books for the eye dissection and I wrote my number in it. I thought I'd leave you a little something of my own. I didn't think it would go unnoticed," I say, laughing at the fact he never saw my gesture.

"I must have been too entranced with the smile on your beautiful face to notice this one," he says, his own beautiful smile, shining at me.

"Next time I'll put your note in the sky so you can't miss it," I tell him, which has both of us laughing. When we quieten down I say, "I meant it Tate, your heart really did save me."

"I love you," he says, before taking my lips with his and showing me how much he loves me through his touch.

Don't Fade. Breathe Easy.

Chapter 25
~

-- Tate --

Tamsyn and I received top marks for our assignments and I couldn't have been happier. Her words struck me right in the heart and I didn't think I could feel anymore for this special girl than I already did but I do.

The last few weeks of school are a blur filled with revision and studying. We have a lot more study group sessions at Tamsyn's in the lead up to exams and even those are a blur. I'm just glad they are over with now.

As we are all seated in the school hall for our graduation ceremony I can't help but feel lost. I don't know what the future holds and it is a scary thought. My parents arrived earlier this week to attend the ceremony and I was happy to see them after so long. They look a lot happier themselves since Tamsyn and I visited them last.

Awards are given out and the main one for the school dux is awarded last. It goes to the student who has achieved the highest grades across their six authority subjects.

Principal Astle says, "And the winner for the school dux is Scott Porter." Our group of friends erupt into cheers at seeing one of our own get the most prestigious award. He deserved it, we know how much he's worked to get it. I cheer as loud as I can for the first person apart from JP and Rafe, who was kind enough to befriend me. And I like to think that we will stay friends in the future, no matter where our paths lead us. Scott also gets handed a fully paid scholarship to the law school he chose to apply to. It is across the country but I'm sure we will manage to stay friends. I couldn't be prouder of my friend for all he's achieved.

As the graduation ceremony comes to an end, we all leap from our seats, excited that this time of our lives is over and we are moving into adulthood. Even if we don't know what that entails. I push through the crowd and find the girl who has my heart. Her head moves back and forth, her eyes searching for something. When she lands on me, her face lights up and she runs to my open arms which lift her up.

With her looking down at me smiling, I say, "We did it. School's over now," breathing out in relief. I lower her down to her feet as she laughs.

"Well not for the ones of us that are going to University, it's not," she says, lightly.

"So you're still thinking of applying to University?" I ask.

"Yeah I think so. Penny got into the entry level health studies course. She told me before the ceremony started and I know Rafe was thinking of looking into Psychology which had interested me too."

"I still don't know what to do," I tell her, dropping my gaze.

"You'll figure it out," she tells me. "Come on, let's go see the others before I have to go to dinner with Mum."

Back at JP's place, I take a moment in my room to think of Quinn and how she would have been today if she was graduating. I pull out her journal I now keep in my bedside table and flick through it. I usually let my fingers flick the pages, stopping when I get a feeling to. I let myself believe it's Quinn directing me to something she thinks I need to see. This time my fingers land on a page I haven't seen before. It says 'bucket list' and while most of the other pages are in either blue or black pen, this has been written in bright coloured markers.

I scan the list of items she has numbered from one to fifty. At first my face brightens with a smile at the thought of Quinn wanting to do these things. The list consists of stuff like bungee jumping, riding a gondola in Venice, lying on a beach in Greece and climbing the Eiffel tower. But as soon as that smile arrives, it is ripped away because Quinn will never get to do any of these things and the thought brings an ache to my chest. I close my eyes wishing this list had been enough to make her stay. I feel like I will forever be asking the question of why couldn't she have stayed.

"Tate, dinner's ready," my mum says, as she knocks on my bedroom door. I close the journal, leaving it on the bed and follow Mum to the kitchen where JP and his parents are seated. My dad brings the meat in from the barbeque for our celebration dinner.

"So boys, before we start eating, we just wanted to say how proud we are of both of you. We know it hasn't been the easiest time for either of you this year but we are so proud you stuck with it and finished," Dad says, to both JP and I.

"Thanks Dad," I say. I look at my mum who has unshed tears in her eyes.

"Aww Mum, it's okay," I say, trying to soothe her so she won't cry.

"I'm okay, I promise. I just need to say something," she admits, taking a deep breath before continuing. "So your father and I had always planned a big trip for you and Quinn after you graduated," she says, wiping away a tear that drips down. "Sadly we don't have Quinn with us but I talked to Sharon and Todd and they thought it would be a good idea if we did a big family trip. All of us together." She leans over the table and hands JP and I an envelope each. We look at each other then don't waste time and rip into them, unfolding the paper and reading.

"Italy?" we both let out excited yells at the same time, which has our parents laughing.

"Yes. We thought we could do a month long trip to celebrate graduating before you have to decide what to do next." I look to JP and he holds his hand up for a high five which I return.

"When do we leave?" JP asks.

"Next week," my dad says, and my heart flits to Tamsyn. I'd have to leave her for a month. He must notice the thought cross my face because he adds, "It would be a month son, and that is only a fraction of time in the grand scheme of things." Then he winks at me. My parents know how much Tamsyn means to me. I left my home to move back to be with her.

"This is so awesome. Thanks everyone," JP tells his parents and mine. We start our meal and I retreat into myself, lost in my thoughts. It isn't until after dinner when I disappear to my room that I notice Quinn's journal, sitting where I left it on my bed. I pick it up and flick back to where her bucket list is, scanning until I find the one I noticed before. Number four: Ride a gondola in Venice. I could do that for her. Then my thoughts grow and I wonder if it's possible if I could complete her whole bucket list. And that thought alone settles something in my heart, like that's what I'm meant to do.

But to do that, I'd have to leave Tamsyn behind. Dad's words replay in my mind, 'it's only a fraction of time in the grand scheme of things.' I need to talk to Tamsyn. Jumping off my bed, I slide my sneakers on and run over to Tamsyn's with Quinn's journal in my hand.

Tanya answers the door, smiling at me.

"She's in her room," she tells me, and I race up the stairs to find

Tamsyn lying in her bed, freshly washed hair, watching T.V. My appearance at her door has her brows pulling in.

"Tate? I thought you were spending the night with your parents?" she asks, confused.

"I was but something happened and I needed to talk to you," I say, sitting next to her on her bed, taking her hands in mine then telling her what happened. "My parents, JP and I and his parents are going on a month long family trip to Italy to celebrate us graduating."

"That's amazing, Tate. That sounds like so much fun," she says, her smile shining at me. I flick through the journal finding the page and showing her the bucket list.

"What's this?" she asks, reading over it.

"It's a bucket list Quinn wrote," I say, her eyes lift to mine, brows furrowed again. I take a deep breath and say, "I feel like I need to fulfill it for her." She looks back down at the list and reads over everything. I see it when she realises what I'm saying. The list is long and it would take me more than a month to tick them all off.

When her eyes raise to mine they're closed while she takes deep breaths, "You're gonna be gone longer than a month, aren't you?" and her shimmering eyes stare at me.

"Would you come with me? We could do it together?" I rush the words, but the moment I say them, I know I want her by my side. I don't know if I can handle being away from her for so long.

She lets out a breath before saying, "I can't leave my mum, Tate. I'm all she has now and I don't want her being left alone in this house. She may seem like she's fine but it's still so raw for both of us," she says.

"I understand. If my parents didn't have each other, I wouldn't have left them either," I sadly say.

"You should do it though. I can see it in your eyes Tate. It's something you need to do and I won't be the one to stand in your way," she says, as a tear escapes.

"I don't wanna leave you," I say, my own eyes burning.

"I know. I don't want you to go but if I had a list like that of my dad's, there isn't anything in this world that would stop me from doing it. I have a feeling it will give you closure and bring you closer to Quinn," she says, softly. I press my forehead to hers and we both close our eyes, breathing the other in.

"It's okay, Tate. Anyway, best friends don't break up, you know," she says, opening her eyes as I do.

We stare at each other for a minute before I take her lips in mine, needing this moment.

-- Tamsyn --

The day has arrived. Today Tate is leaving. The others and I have gathered at JP's house to wish them farewell. Tate told me he talked to his parents and they were a bit hesitant to let him go, so they are going to carry on with him after JP and his parents leave for another few weeks and then Tate will be on his own. Backpacking and taking any jobs he can, until he can fulfill Quinn's list.

I was upset when he told me his plans but I know deep in my heart what I said was true. I would have done the same if my dad had a list. It's a way for him to feel closer to Quinn and I love him too much to deny him that. I could be selfish and beg him to stay but I don't want him to resent me. Life is too short for regrets and I could see it in Tate's eyes, he would regret it if he didn't do this. They say if you love something to set it free and I love Tate with all I have, so there was never an option of trying to make him stay.

Letting him go again is going to be hard, but unlike last time, this time my heart is full. I love this boy more than I ever thought I could love someone and even though we will be apart, I'd rather know he was happy doing something without me than with me, wishing he was somewhere else.

"Okay everyone, the Ubers are nearly here to take us to the airport so we better start saying our goodbyes," JP's dad says, so everyone starts hugging each other.

"I'm a phone call away if you need me bro," I hear JP say to Rafe quietly.

"I know dude. I'm good, I promise," Rafe replies, as they hug it out.

I say bye to Tate's parents and JP and then I turn to Tate. It's as if we left each other until last on purpose. Putting off saying goodbye until the last possible moment.

"We might just take our bags outside," I hear Tate's mum say, as they all try to give Tate and I a moment alone. When it's just the two of us alone, I rush into his arms, clinging to him as the tears unleash.

"Shhh it's okay, Sweetness," he tells me, his voice cracking. I breathe in his earthy scent, tucking this moment away in my memories.

"Make sure you look after yourself," I mumble, as my body shakes. He cups my cheeks firmly and raises my eyes to his.

"I need you to remember that there is nowhere I can go that my heart will not love you," he confesses, which makes the tears flood down faster.

"I know," I reply, as he kisses me deeply.

"It's not goodbye, it's just see you later," he tells me, staring into my eyes, speaking his truth.

"I'll see you later then," I whisper, as I hiccup.

"I'll call you every night," he says, and I nod. "I love you."

"I love you too," I reply, and he pulls me back into his arms, squeezing me. Then he releases me, kisses my forehead and with tears in his eyes, he turns and walks out the door.

"Look after her for me," I hear him say.

"Always," I hear Rafe reply. My knees buckle and I fall to the ground, sobbing as I let the other half of my heart go. It feels like hours later but it's only minutes when I'm lifted into strong arms, letting out all my sadness.

"Come on Petal, let's get you home," Rafe says, holding me tightly. "Scott, grab the key and lock the door dude. I gotta look after the house while they are gone," he says to Scott, as he carries me out the door.

"We're here for you Tam, whenever you need us," Penny says, as we walk to my house while Rafe carries me effortlessly.

He places me in my bed, and we settle down for a sleepover, while they let me cry and miss the only boy my heart wants. Penny stays in the bed with me, holding my hand the whole time. Once the others are asleep, Rafe walks over to sit by me. He pulls a small folded piece of paper out of his pocket, handing it to me with a sad smile. I open it up and the tears start again. It's a note from Tate. He's drawn two footprints with the words, 'my feet will always lead me back to you.' Rafe pulls me back into his arms, hugging me tightly while I fall apart.

Epilogue

One year later

-- Tamsyn --

With the weight of my textbooks I've just purchased, securely in my new backpack, I follow the path to take us to the library. The hustle and bustle of orientation is overwhelming to say the least. Even with it being my second year at University, the amount of people on campus is a lot to get used to. Nerves get the better of me as Penny and I wait in line for our new student IDs. They have a system worked out so they process them fast and the ID is ready in a matter of minutes. When I'm handed mine, I visibly cringe as Penny peers over my shoulder and lets out a cackle at my expense.

"It's even worse than last year," I tell her, deflating.

"Who cares, it's not Uni unless you have a crappy ID photo, right?" she says, trying to make me feel better as we wait for hers. When she gets handed hers a minute later, my mouth drops open.

"Of course you'd say that when your photo is flawless," I accuse, staring at the perfect smiling face of Penny which she holds in her hands. This only makes her laugh more.

"Come on, let's go meet JP over by the club sign up stalls. You think you'll sign up for anything this year?" she asks, leading us to the front of campus where they usually set up all the stalls.

"You think there will be anything worth signing up for?" I ask.

"Who knows, but we're Uni students. The world is our oyster. It's time to dream big dreams and all that garbage," she says, which has us both laughing.

"That's the same speech you gave me last year," I tell her, clutching my stomach.

"Maybe I need to mix it up as you didn't sign up for anything last year. The speech obviously is a dud," she says. "So have you heard from Tate lately?" she asks, as we continue on our way.

"Yeah, the last email he sent he said he was going to travel to France for a bit and then maybe cruise around the Mediterranean. He didn't sound too sure. He's enjoying himself though and that's the main thing. I'm happy for him," I tell her, meaning it. I am happy for him although I miss him terribly. But this past year I've learnt to rely on myself more and it's a great feeling to know I can cope better now. He keeps in touch with phone calls and emails and he seriously sounds like he's been bitten by the travelling bug. I can't blame him, his adventures do sound amazing.

"It's a shame Scott's scholarship has taken him to his fancy law school and not here with us. I do miss not having him around all the time," Penny pouts, and I can't help but feel the same.

"He'll visit when he can next. And with social media these days, it isn't that bad." I tell her.

"True," she says. I glance her way and notice the moment her eyes widen and a huge smile spreads across her face. "There's JP," she says, pointing into the crowd, spotting him looking at different stalls. The

216

moment she gets within range so he can hear her she yells, "JP," which has his head turning our way, with his own goofy smile on his face.

He races over and kisses Penny on the lips, flinging his arm casually around her shoulders. It's great to see them finally so open about their relationship. I know they kept it a secret for so long at school because JP was worried about what would happen to her friendship with me if they broke up, but I always knew they were good for each other.

"You find any good clubs?" I ask.

"Not down this end, they are all political and media groups which don't interest me. Maybe I should join a social sports team," he says, lost in thought.

"Is Rafe around?" I ask, missing him. He convinced his parents to let him live on campus this year and have the whole university experience. We all still worry about Rafe but he's in a much better place now and he's still on his medication and going to therapy regularly.

"He's over in the dorms getting sorted but he said he will meet us here later," JP tells us, as he leads us past the political stalls and down to the other end. Students are everywhere checking out different clubs and getting talked into signing up. You can pick out the newbies by the overwhelmed expressions on their faces. We all had them last year. There's stalls for everything. Baking clubs, writing clubs, drama clubs and even volunteering clubs.

"There's actually a club over there I thought might tickle your fancy Ice Queen," JP says. His use of my old nickname has my own smile widening at him as I follow the direction of his stare. My breath hitches as my feet take me to the club he suggested. The huge black banner with, 'Star Gazing,' written in white, hangs from above.

"Hi there, would you like to sign up?" one of the peppy girls behind the stall asks me, holding out a pen. Before I can second guess myself, I sign my name and number.

"It's just a social thing and we get together randomly too," the other girl says, smiling at me.

"Sounds perfect," I say, my gaze falling to my star bracelet, jingling on my wrist. The bracelet and necklace that I never take off. Under the bracelet on the inside of my wrist, I rub my thumb back and forth over the delicate tattoo I got, right after Tate left. It's the second star he drew for me. The one where he left a gap so I could let the light in. It's been a constant reminder of his words and has helped me when he wasn't around to remind me himself.

Shaking myself out of my thoughts, I return her smile and that's when I feel the familiar prickles at the back of my neck. My breathing picks up as I say goodbye to the girls and turn around, searching the crowd. I scan face after face but I don't see the familiar green eyes or blond hair that I love anywhere. It must just be wishful thinking since he was on my mind.

I'm about to walk off to find JP and Penny when I hear the girl say, "Would you like to sign up?"

"Sure would. Stars always remind me to shine," the deeper but familiar voice says, and as my heart skips a beat, I turn around.

"Well we are happy that you'll be joining us," the peppy girl says, and I catch his breathtaking smile before he turns to face me fully.

"I'm happy I'll be joining you too," he says, as his smile grows, shoulders shrugging at me. His blond hair is now longer and tied up at the nape of his neck and he has a bit of facial hair, neatly trimmed across his jaw and chin, making him look older than I remember. His body has more muscles than he did back in school. He looks like a man now instead of the boy who left.

"You're here?" I ask, unbelieving.

"Didn't I tell you my feet would always lead me back to you, Sweetness," Tate says, and I lurch myself at him, wrapping my arms and legs around him tightly. Laughing, he catches me effortlessly.

218

"You enrolled?" I ask him, still not believing he's here.

"Yeah I managed to get in with a late enrollment," he says, staring into my eyes.

"What about travelling and finishing Quinn's bucket list?" I ask.

"I think Quinn would be more than happy with what I managed to accomplish over the past year. Plus the stars aren't the same without you by my side," he says, and I can't help the sigh that escapes my lips. He reaches up, while holding me with one hand and grabs my wrist from around his neck. He must have noticed my new tattoo which I never mentioned to him. He brings it to his lips with a soft smile gracing his face. "I love you," he softly says.

"I love you, more," I return, closing the distance with my lips and kissing the only guy my heart will ever love, knowing he feels exactly the same. My first love and last love, all wrapped up in one.

As we break apart he says, "So I guess that makes us two percenters," with his blinding smile directed at me.

I tilt my head to the side, confused, "Huh?" I say.

"You once said only two percentage of high school relationships last so that puts us in the two percent, because from this day on, I'm never leaving you again," he says, which fills my heart.

"Is that so?" I tease.

"It is," he says, looking into my eyes and I nod, seeing the truth in his eyes.

-- Tate --

Damn I missed this girl. Travelling around Europe and ticking off things on Quinn's list was great but there was always a niggling feeling that something was missing. That something I'm now holding in my arms. My mind wanders to Quinn and I know she would have loved to have seen everything I did but she would also want me to be happy. And since she's been gone, I haven't been able to find true happiness unless Tamsyn is with me.

It's still hard living without her and having happy moments where I wish she was here. I know Quinn loved me and she would want me to be happy and living my life, so that's what I'm trying to do. I still grieve for Quinn but as time goes on, the grief changes. It started as an overwhelming consuming void that I was drowning in and I had to work to pull myself out of. Now it's still there, it's just more of a low thumping feeling in my heart that occasionally gets triggered but which I can handle. They say time heals all wounds but I feel this is one wound that will forever be open, never fully healed and occasionally weeping. I did lose a part of myself when she died and I don't think I've ever really gotten it back, nor do I want it, if it means I can feel connected to her still.

Grief may have been the foundation of my relationship with Tamsyn but it's not what kept us coming back to each other. Love does that. Love keeps pulling us back together. It was hard to leave her behind and go on my overseas adventure, pursuing a dream that was Quinn's and not mine. I felt I owed it to Quinn to fulfill it for her since she never got the chance to do it herself. She never got to see the amazing sights she dreamt of and every time I checked one off her list, I wished she would have held on for that list. I wish she could have seen how much there was to live for. The list in turn started to weigh on me and I knew I had to start living for myself instead of following Quinn's dream. I had my own dream to pursue. Tamsyn. Quinn would understand. She would want me to follow my heart.

I meant it when I said my feet would always lead me back to Tamsyn. My feet and my heart. It's as if she holds a part of my soul and whenever we've been apart too long, she tugs on that part and it draws me back to her. Like magic. For the rest of my days no matter what, I'll always let my feet lead me back to her, because that's where I belong. With my magical green fairy. My Sweetness.

The End!

Rafe's story

COMING SOON!!!

Don't Fade. Breathe Easy.

Notes from the Author

Wow. What a journey Tate and Tamsyn have taken me on. If you've read this far I hope I did their story justice. This story was born from the grief I experienced at losing my dad, my sister and one of my best friends Jonathon, all within the span of ten months in 2019.

It is incredibly hard to grieve for one person let alone three all within a short time frame. Every day there are thoughts of each of them that will flit through my mind. Or some days I will be consumed with thoughts of one of them and then the next moment, it will be one of the others. So my mind at times can turn into a pile of mush from thoughts of them.

After Jonathon committed suicide, I needed something else to help me cope and I found an outlet by writing letters to them. It was this way of coping that led to my story forming. So I do mean it when I say that this story would have never come about without them. It just pains me that they aren't here to read it themselves.

I know that sometimes in Tate and Tamsyn's journeys, there is a lot of pain and heartache. If it resonated with you because of your own loss, I thank you for continuing to read because it means I am not alone in how I feel in my grief. I hope you enjoyed the connection between Tate and Tamsyn. Every person deserves someone who sees through them and sees their soul inside, especially when that soul is screaming for help. I hope if you haven't already that, you find your own Tate or Tamsyn to spend your life with.

I know most of you fell in love with Rafe as much as I did and wanted to hear more of his story. This trilogy was the story of Tate and Tamsyn and Rafe deserves his own time in the spotlight so I've written his story in a separate book. His story will be released shortly and it will hopefully cure your curiosity about Rafe and answer any lingering questions you may have about him.

Thank you again for taking a chance on me as it isn't easy on an indie author starting out. If you liked these books, follow me on Facebook, Instagram and Goodreads to keep up to date with new releases as I have more books to come. And please leave a review as it would mean so much to me as it does help.

Remember to keep shining and let the light in.

Buckets of love, Sarah Delany xx

Acknowledgements

To Rebecca Andrews and Michael Pati Fuiava, thank you so much for sticking with me and helping me make decisions. You've been the backbone of this journey for me and I wouldn't have gotten this far without you two to help me along. I will forever be indebted to you.

To Mum and Wayne Ayers, thank you for reading my story and encouraging me as well as offering feedback. Your thoughts helped my books reach another level and I can't thank you enough. Sorry for all the tears my emotions on paper have caused you.

To the members of my launch team. The ones who were with me for book one, book two or all three, you are truly wonderful for taking the time to read and review my books. As well as all the sharing of posts. I couldn't have done it without you. Kylie Fraser, Germayne, Lena, Chrys, Connie, Rita, Sarah Jackson, Donna, Kitan, Bumbum, Naz, Kylie Malota, Matt Froggatt and Rochelle, I am honoured to have had you on this journey with me. It has meant the world to me.

To TJ and our boys, I love you more than you will probably ever know and I couldn't be any more blessed than to do this crazy journey of life with you all. TJ, you are my very own Tate xx.

Don't Fade. Breathe Easy.

Playlist for 'Don't Fade. Breathe Easy'

1. True Colours by Anna Kendrick and Justin Timberlake
2. Everybody Hurts by R.E.M
3. Through the Rain by Mariah Carey
4. When I Look at You by Miley Cyrus
5. Yesterday by Leona Lewis
6. Fight Song by Rachel Platten
7. Never Give Up on Us by Connie Talbot
8. Never Not by Lauv
9. 10,000 Hours by Dan + Shay with Justin Bieber
10. Rainbow by Casey Musgraves
11. Better Together by Jack Johnson
12. You Set My World on Fire by Loving Caliber and Selestine
13. Love Me Like You Do by Ellie Goulding
14. Marvin Gaye by Charlie Puth and Meghan Trainor
15. Wild Things by Alessia Cara
16. I Wanna Dance With Somebody by Whitney Houston
17. Graduation (Friends Forever) by Vitamin C
18. Bless the Broken Road by Rascal Flatts
19. Falling Like the Stars by James Arthur
20. All of the Stars by Ed Sheeran
21. 11:11 by Jae Jin
22. Home by Michael Buble

https://spoti.fi/33zra7E

Don't Fade. Breathe Easy.

Feedback

Did you enjoy this book? Would you like to give feedback? Did you know word of mouth is what makes the publishing world go round. If you enjoyed reading this book, please feel free to share your opinions or post a review online on Amazon, Goodreads or even on my Facebook page. We would love to hear from you. Or even better, let your facebook friends know and encourage them to read the book.

Check out my Facebook and Instagram or feel free to email me.

sarahdelany.com

@sarahdelanywrites

sarahdelanywrites@gmail.com

Don't Fade. Breathe Easy.

About the Author

'Don't Fade. Breathe Easy' is Sarah Delany's third novel and is the final book in the TNT trilogy. Her next release will be a spin off about the character of Rafe from the TNT Trilogy.

She is one of eight siblings, has a loving partner and is a stay at home mother to their four young boys. Writing this novel was a therapeutic way for Sarah to deal with the pain and grief she suffered in 2019 after losing not only her father but also her sister and one of her best friends. She's a New Zealander who currently resides in Brisbane, Australia.

Don't Fade. Breathe Easy.